# TOMMASO AND THE
# BLIND PHOTOGRAPHER

GESUALDO BUFALINO was born at Comiso, Sicily, in 1920. He studied literature at Catania and Palermo, and was a teacher by profession, turning author only after his retirement in 1976. He started his first novel, *The Plague-spreader's Tale*, in 1950, but it was only in 1981, after he had taken the discarded manuscript out of the drawer at the prompting of his fellow-Sicilian writer Leonardo Sciascia and reworked it, that it was published; it won the Campiello Prize. It was soon followed by *Blind Argus*, then by *Night's Lies*, which won the prestigious Strega Prize. All three novels are published by Harvill, as also a collection of short stories, *The Keeper of Ruins*. Bufalino died in 1996, leaving the present novel, *Tommaso and the Blind Photographer*, for posthumous publication.

PATRICK CREAGH won the John Florio Prize for his translation of *Blind Argus*. In addition to his translation of *Night's Lies, The Keeper of Ruins*, and *The Plague-spreader's Tale* he has brought to an English-language readership the work of many leading Italian writers, including Brancati, Vassalli, Magris, Morazzoni, Satta, Ortese and Tabucchi. He is also a considerable poet in his own right.

*Gesualdo Bufalino*

# TOMMASO AND THE BLIND PHOTOGRAPHER

*Translated from the Italian by
Patrick Creagh*

THE HARVILL PRESS
LONDON

First published in Italy with the title *Tommaso e il fotografo cieco*
by Bompiani, Milan, 1996

First published in Great Britain in 2000 by
The Harvill Press
2 Aztec Row
Berners Road
London N1 0PW

www.harvill.com

1 3 5 7 9 8 6 4 2

A CIP catalogue record for this book
is available from the British Library

ISBN 1 86046 568 4

Designed and typeset in Galliard by
Libanus Press, Marlborough, Wiltshire

Printed and bound in Great Britain by
Butler & Tanner Ltd at Selwood Printing, Burgess Hill

# CONTENTS

1   Compass Bearings                                    1

2   A Walk with Tir                                     6

3   The Mouse-hunt                                     14

4   Round the Houses                                   27

5   In Actual Fact                                     43

6   Strange Doings in the Building                     54

7   The Get-together                                   67

8   My Prison Life                                     78

9   The Funeral                                        86

10  Manoeuvres, Agitations, Negotiations               98

11  The Filibuster                                    112

12  Firstfruits of Revelation                         126

13  Hunt-the-thimble                                  140

14  On the Top of the World and
    From There on Down                                152

15  The Crunch                                        165

16  Epiprologue                                       177

    *Dramatis personae*                               184

# ONE

# Compass Bearings

When I was a lad I loved the sound of the rain. Especially in the drowsiness of early morning when among the vapours of an iron-grey dream I would hear it enter my ears with the hubbub of an aviary, or else mimic the tramping of feet, many feet, as in a long march or a stampede for the lifeboats.

"Here we go, it's raining!" I heard a voice soundlessly tell me. Nothing more than a simple statement, but enough to arouse me to a state of happy restlessness, a kind of demisting of the senses . . . And these, already free of the phantoms of night, offered to the first dawning of consciousness a calm though fervent cleansing of mind. I knew that it was time to get up, to wash and dress, but I was too tempted to go on playing for a while with the last bickerings between raindrops and window-panes, attuning their cadences to an inner music of my own, now headlong, now stately, at times resembling rock music and at others a sung Mass. Until I found myself sitting on the edge of the bed conducting an invisible orchestra with two small hands half engulfed in their pyjama sleeves. Meanwhile the rain had stopped, and on the floor a newborn sun was busy drawing many staves of light through the slats of the shutters. I was older by one day and happy about it.

Many years have passed since then. Nowadays I pay no attention to weather either good or bad. I notice only the stripes

of light with which the one of them ravishes me while the other
deprives me of. Here where I live, in a poky semi-basement, there
is only an apology for a window, a mere slit between wall and
ceiling barred this way and that and shut off when I want it by
a curtain. A tiny belvedere, after all, since it looks out at street
level and provides a providential gap in the plastered wall which
separates me from the outside world. So low is the ceiling that
it only takes a stack of three dictionaries and there I am, my
head level with the pavement and ready to enjoy the sights.

It may be no great shakes as a show, but it's varied, non-stop
and free of charge. I watch a parade of battalions of trouser-
legs, skirts, jeans, perambulators and dogs on leads, the tips of
umbrellas and parasols . . . the netherest limbs of men and of
women, more of women than men, of unknown women on
whose cellulitis, plaster casts, varicosities, shadowy cavities and
shapely eminences I never tire of pondering. Unless it be that a
gust of wind sticks a wafted page of newspaper onto my viewing
screen and blinds me. A matter of seconds, then the spyhole
clears of its own accord and is peopled once more with enticing
moving pictures.

So you well may ask how I live, how I keep alive, and how I've
come to end up here. From a certain finesse of style you may
have scented the fact that I have had my whack of education
but in addition to that I am pretty swollen-headed (how can
it be otherwise with a fellow who writes about nothing but
himself?); that I like to orate in rolling, rounded periods (I
formed this habit to show off to a woman and have never lost
it); and that to my nosiness I add a pinch of cynicism, the
indispensable endowment of any novelist.

But first things first. If you ask around the place you will be
told that my uppitiness is just pique, that I'm nothing but a
poor old suffering Job, turfed out of my profession, abandoned

by my wife, a heavy drinker but a light-fingered fellow in the supermarkets.

I don't deny it. But let's get things in order.

My name is Tommaso Mulè, I am forty-nine years old and I am, or am thought to be, a trifle weak in the head. I'll tell you how it all started. It was one morning as I stood shaving before the bathroom mirror and regarding my ageing face – a yellow leaf afloat at the bottom of a bucket of crystal-clear water. At that moment I was assailed by the most insignificant and apparently ephemeral of questions: "So what?" I didn't know how to answer, of course, but when I left the house I was aware of an uneasiness that stayed with me like a crumb stuck between the teeth. Even later, in the course of a day, sitting at the computer or on the loo, or even making love if occasion offered, my head rang with the questioning bell-tones, "So what? So what? So what?" I realized that from then on I could never again live so much as a minute without being gnawed at, like a worm-eaten fruit, by what in inkhorn terms I persuaded myself to call "mental reservation". I would go to the theatre, or I'd read a book, and all the while I'd be thinking, "So what?" And they'd calm me down, or they'd bawl me out, take me by the arm and talk politics, or sport . . . and I pretended to agree, I said yes or no, I got angry or blushed as the case might be. But never without feeling a silent, insistent "BUT" prick me under my skin, the leastest particle of a thought that couldn't yet be put into words, except for those few sad niggardly syllables such as "But I . . .", or "But if . . .", or "So what?"

An obsession accompanied – according to my wife – by the nervous little smile, ironic perhaps, or perhaps just stupid (said she) of one who thinks himself the craftiest fellow on earth and keeps watch on life's little tricks through the eyeholes of a carnival mask. Things being this way I was bound to lose my friends, my acquaintances, my job. Without too many regrets, to tell the truth, as for my ultimate revenge I pondered on the umpteenth mental reservation that I would cast in the teeth of death on the last day: "So what?"

Since then I have found a home here, in the basement of this block of flats, acting as general dogsbody. It sounds like nothing, but it isn't: it's a shouldering of responsibility after such a slavish and insipid career as a journalist. It's my job, in fact, to collect the rent from all the tenants, which involves making out a notice for each one, putting them into the same number of letterboxes, writing out the receipts, adding up the payments and finally handing them over to the lawyer and chief administrator of the property, Leone Mundula, who more or less trusts my accounting. He knows that if it weren't for this place I would die, that too obvious an error would cost me my job and therefore my life . . . Nor do my duties stop short at rent-collecting. I have other more everyday tasks: minor repairs to the plumbing and wiring, checking the supply of heating oil to make sure it doesn't run out during the cold weather, thus leaving this whole Escurial of a building out under the frosty stars . . . replacing lightbulbs in the lifts and corridors . . .

What do I get out of it? A modest regular wage and free lodging, which is shabby enough in all conscience, but there you are: every castaway gets attached to his own rock. And in addition a few trifling details of management enable me to make an occasional profit. As when I take an imperceptible rake-off on the money for supplies of toilet paper and detergent, or cadge Christmas or Easter presents, or shut my eyes to the shortcomings of Adele and Santina, the cleaning-women, in exchange for impromptu attentions in the service room among the brooms and dusters . . . Nothing more nor less than anyone would do in my place. Finally – and it is the supreme benefit – in the endless and salutary repetition of every act, in the sublime routine of duty, I have discovered an infallible remedy for the nightly torment of a lifetime. In other words, against all odds, I have vanquished insomnia.

# TWO

# A Walk with Tir

*Thursday August 10th*

Someone at the door. I know who it is even before he enters. He has knocked with the metal ferule of his stick, so it is Tiresias, the blind photographer. I say Tiresias, but that is the name I have bestowed on him to raise his status. To be strictly accurate his name is Bartolomeo, Bar to his familiars; or more familiarly still, to me he is Tir. With all the stupid puns involved when, massive as he is, he knocks over a piece of furniture or a pile of books, in emulation of the vast juggernauts, the dinosaurs of the road. In a word, one of the few friends I have in this immense block of flats.

In reply to my "come in" he pushes open the door and feels his way forward, delving his stick into the air like an oar into water. He knows that from the doorway to my table means five steps down and nine paces forward, and he negotiates them with all the confidence and caution of a tightrope walker. Then he stops at the spot where intuition tells him that an empty chair awaits him. He is preceded by a violent wave of eau-de-cologne, which he has a weakness for.

"So how did it go this morning, Tir? Good hunting?"

"Not a thing. I didn't see a soul. One client I was expecting called up to cancel. Cesare is away on holiday, and I need your help."

Cesare is the guide-boy, on loan from the College of the Divine Zeal, a seventeen-year-old orphan who leads Tir around, sets up his equipment, describes the faces, the landscapes, the possible shots, details to him the qualities of the light and shade. Because here is the paradox of it: at the age of fifty or more Tiresias, formerly a famous portraitist and author of nudes for "Playboy", until blinded by a glaucoma seven years ago, still obstinately sticks to his profession. With some fairly surprising results, it must be said. At his place there is a constant stream of successful women who, weary of adoring themselves in the mirror, hanker after less fleeting images to donate to their lovers.

When one of these ladies visits him Tir very properly shoos away the boy before inviting her to undress and stretch out on an ottoman or a leopardskin dating from the 1930s. It has become quite the fashion with rising starlets and well-heeled housewives to come and expose themselves before his sightless eyes, while on his side he fires off one exposure after another. Occasionally, to reassure the more reluctant, Tir summons Matilde to his assistance. Matilde is his much younger sister, who lives with him in a two-bedroom flat on the third floor. A girl with legs like beams of light, short red curly hair and wide, ravenous eyes that seem set on adding to their booty of visible targets the portion unfairly stolen from her brother. Not, on the whole, a great beauty, but embellished with mysterious silences. She has a habit of vanishing for days on end, throwing him into fits of anxiety, and then reappearing with a touch of radiance in her gait and gestures. Today is one of the days when she is not to be found, and Tiresias has come to ask for help.

"Come and help me look for her. I know the bar she goes to," says he, with that disconsolate pout that I find irresistible – and all the more maddening for that. And I make heavy weather of refusing, countering with my now legendary cloistered life, my horror of venturing out among the crowds, the shops, the traffic . . .

"Yours," he rebukes me, "is a dummy-life, you've reduced yourself to the status of an earthworm. I can't judge your face, but I bet it's chalk-white. It'll do you good to let your nose peel in the sun for once."

Could he be right? But however reluctantly I set off. Not without reminding him with a pinch of spite that if mine is a dummy-life then his habit of seeing by proxy is dummy-sight, and more deplorable still. He would do better, there in his darkness, to submit to the customs of the blind: eye-drops, walks with the dog, books in Braille . . .

An oft-repeated homily to which he reacts with a burst of defiance: "It's my Nikon that sees for me. My camera is my eyes, my hands, my . . . " He breaks off, knowing I can't stand smut. But he starts off again at once with twice as much vehemence: "With every flash I regain an instant of lost sunshine. I deliver an object or an event from its destiny of perdition, and whilst I myself submit to time I snatch a prey from its jaws. I ratify a death, but I immobilize it in an immortal effigy . . . "

All declamations I have heard from his lips more than once, a rigmarole that appeared in the catalogue of a show of his work in his heyday. I am therefore very careful not to give him any rope. On the contrary, I hasten to take him by the arm and help him to retrace his steps to the doorway.

Outside it's a swelter. Not a soul in what we glorify by the name of "the Corso" as far as the eye can see. Dazzled by the sun I totter and darned near vomit. The asphalt beneath my sandals like live coals. He passes over it with the tread of an angel, beneath a straw hat that fits him like a halo, immaculate in white linen, disfigured only by his dark glasses, their sombre protest against the light.

We are alone in the desert of the city and I tell him so, but all the same he lowers his voice: "Matilde," he says, "ought to be your concern as well. She's a woman and a half, and you haven't had a woman at all since Rosa left you."

This too is an old, old story. Tir is always terrified that his sister will leave him in the lurch and never come back. If she were to link her lot with mine he would have a perpetual guarantee of proximity and assistance. He lowers his voice still further: "I ought not to confess it to you, but when I still had the use of my eyes I acted the Peeping Tom with Matilde. Now don't misunderstand me. I never went any further than enjoying the sight of her. So that when she was still quite little I often caught her with my lens while she was sleeping naked. And I have gone on doing so now that I am blind, without her suspecting. Some afternoons, now that the heat makes her strip off, as soon as I hear the deep breathing of sleep in her room I creep in barefoot and take her picture."

"That's rape," I comment icily. "Aggravated by incest."

"Nothing of the sort," he retorts. "A dummy-rape, a dummy-incest, if anything. Like your life, like my sight, like everything else. Everything in the world is a stand-in, a prosthesis, a fiddle of some sort, be it dyed hair, false teeth or verbal artifice.

"This," he concludes, triumphantly brandishing his black Nikon, "this and this alone never lies . . . " And after a pause, "Are you astonished? Are you scandalized?"

In the interests of good manners I say that I am, though in fact there are far worse exploits flaunted in today's paper, under banner headlines.

Tir continues: "If I have to level with you all the way, I must tell you I'm confessing this for a purpose, in fact two. The first is, that by showing you Matilde in her birthday suit I'm hoping to get you to lust after her. The other is that I need an accomplice to retrieve these negatives and prints. I simply can't involve Cesare in this negligible perversion of mine."

"Whereas me you can?" I retort, anxious lest his pushiness breach those ramparts that for better or worse I have made my fortress, and disturb the status quo of my frail routine. As he doesn't answer, but simply pulls a wry face, I hazard a guess at his feelings. I think he's already sorry for his outburst. Not that he doesn't trust me, but because of the ticklish matter of giving me the upper hand by revealing his shameful secret. Already in his pride he is suffering more from my accomplice silence than from any vituperation even I could lavish on him. In any case, we mutually reach a painful impasse.

We cross the road. The bar he mentions is only a few blocks away. An occasional pedestrian is now seen to emerge from the haze of dust. An optimistic taxi slows up beside one after another, gives them a brief glance and steps on the gas without waiting for an answer. As for us, he ignores us altogether, we must strike him as two tramps moving hedge. Odd this because, if I am not, at least Tir is properly dressed, even to his suede moccasins and knee-length socks.

"In this bar," he resumes glibly, "Matilde is at home, she's a friend of the owner, sometimes she even stays overnight. The owner is an elderly woman and doesn't like to be on her own."

I don't believe a word of it but persist in holding my tongue. In any case we have now arrived at a metal shutter rolled firmly down, padlocked at the bottom and bearing the legend "Closed for holiday". I tell him this but he won't give in: "They'll have gone to the sea together, very likely. However, just a phone call would have . . . "

"Come off it, you know how girls are . . . " Thus I attempt to comfort him as I drag him off towards the second Station of the Cross, the photographic laboratory run by Domenico Cuffaro

& Son at the corner of Via Cialdini. But before that, as I catch sight of our two shadows stunted by the midday sun, "Tir," I suggest, "take a couple of shots downwards, towards our feet." And I explain what I want from him.

By some miracle the shop has the shutters halfway up, and in the semi-darkness within an assistant is filing her nails. When I hand over the receipt and she returns with the prints, her expression hovers between disgust and the giggles . . . She must have taken a peek at the negatives.

When I join him outside my blind friend blurts out: "Have a look at them, they're yours, I promised you them. However, when you look at them you must give me an exact description of each one."

My low spirits sink all the lower. I have my doubts about his real intentions. I seem to be left holding the baby in some childish, not to say sinister, scheme of his. Is he exploiting me, and my eyesight, to vouch for the success of his secret incursions? A confirmation, is that what he's after? A medal for self-abasement to vindicate his helpless plight? Or perhaps that's not how things are, and even worse awaits me.

Just so. Stripping off the cellophane wrapper I find that Tir has not been taking me for a sucker. The shot is indeed that of Matilde, starkers and asleep, with a surprising alertness in the features, the set of the jaw, the perspiring brow. As if suddenly stricken with terror she bunches one fist against her bush and spreads another hand to cover an immature breast. "Pretty, eh?" says Tir at my side as I comment on the prints. Which for the most part are good, though occasionally out of focus or out of frame. I get to the second to last of them and here my voice fails me. Because it shows Matilde awake, her eyes wide open, fixed on the camera, and on her lips a laugh . . . A laugh at the same time of agonized humiliation and sombre joy. So Matilde knew. She may not always have done so, but certainly on this occasion she knew and said nothing. Allowing her brother to perform his ritual depravity, be it out of contempt, or pity, or love . . .

But that is not all. The conclusion has a further shock in store for me. In the last shot, taken at a different hour of a different day and in different light conditions, Matilde is really asleep, her mouth heavy and half-open, her body hidden by the sheet except for a triangle of brown thigh. But it must be said that on the same pillow, mingling his curly gypsy locks with her red ringlets, motionless in a coma of satiety, lies the lad Cesare entirely naked down to his adolescent groin. What should I do?

"These two are worthless," I tell him. "The camera moved, I'll tear them up." I put them in my pocket, grip his arm again and pilot him homewards.

"Well?" comes his anxious, pandering voice at my side. "What d'you say? Do you like her?"

"I'll think about it," I say after a slight hesitation, but he has already burst into tears: "She's lost, isn't she? She'll never come back, will she?"

God knows how he has understood, or what he has understood from my hesitation, but certain it is that I feel caught in a trap, with emotions I thought long dead in me; grief, for example, and anger. Not simply for him, for myself, for the woman and the boy who will come back tomorrow or else nevermore, but for all the living and the dead of every clime and time, for the incalculable sum total of their sorrow, the sorrow of the world that swells in the bowels and the heart of God. Who, from the pure empyrean where he sits, enthroned above all height, will surely know the reason why the two of us, Tommaso and Bartolomeo, an ill-matched pair of minuscule ants, are crawling along down here in the furnace of August, in all our listless profanity . . . It is only to him, therefore, that I appeal for an answer to my eternal "So what?" It is only before him that I fall to my knees in the street and yet again protest:

"O why, Your Worship, why?"

# THREE

# The Mouse-hunt

*Sunday, August 13th*

There is a blatant contradiction in my selection of solitudes. As a rule one of solitary disposition goes in search of deserts or mountain tops, in the company of an eagle if he is vain; and if not, in that of a flock of sheep, as we learn from Leopardi. I on the contrary, and despite all tradition, have retreated to an urban, indeed to a metropolitan hermitage, and one which does not exonerate me, as part of my daily duties, from the most ordinary dealings with other people. Without counting the espionage I indulge in from my observation point, which reveals me as still curious and anxious about my fellows. Does this mean that my quarantine is a bluff, a pose? No, that is not the way of it. By disencumbering myself from every civic and family obligation, avoiding every surprise that might occur and consigning myself to a monotony that gladdens me, I have managed to reduce my relations with others to a time-saving exchange of greetings and conventions. For which reason, during my tranquil days of house-arrest, any suggestion of alarm is out of the question, emotional wear and tear is perfectly negligible, and I can live at a cut price amongst people as transient and ephemeral as movie extras. It also helps that there are a crowd of them, and I muddle up their names and faces, thus remaining gloriously extraneous to their personal trials and tribulations. They are shadows, a people of shadows, inhabitants of a city of shadows. In spite of the name, Flower City, as it was baptized by the proprietor (one Mr Cacciola, an Italo-American who lives in Florida and governs us at long distance), or else Shit Building, in the words of Johnny Bisceglie, the most consistently insolvent of all the tenants. In effect Flower City (or Shit Building) is an aborted skyscraper, an Italian-style cloud-cuckoo-land, built on the site of a scruffy shantytown, bought for a handful of dollars and bulldozed to the ground. The original design was for twin towers of twelve storeys each, respectively called "Carnation" and "Sunflower", linked together by fire escapes and flying walkways, between which towers there was to be a continual shuttling of elevators, both goods and passenger. The whole of this eyesore was to be roofed over by an attic two thousand square metres in extent, or rather expansion, already booked by some construction company. And roofing the attic apartment itself was to be a roof-cum-terrace of commensurate dimensions, densely thicketed with parabolic antennae and equipped with coin-in-the-slot telescopes for those desiring close-ups of the many-windowed city or of the distant luminaries of the skies.

This was the big idea, as far as possible conforming to the grandeur of an Hotel Majestic in Palm Beach (though with a few suggestions of Notre Dame, no less) and also the aesthetic tastes of the proprietor, Mr "Jupiter" Cacciola – so nicknamed by his subjects because he thundered from afar with demands for higher rents and threats of eviction. The truth was that, owing to a crisis in his financial dealings in Las Vegas and Wall Street, of his mega-edifice (the papier-mâché model of which is still to be seen under a glass bell in a corner of the entrance hall) very little is actually extant. Only one of the two complexes, the "Carnation", was brought to completion, or almost, while the other, the "Sunflower", has remained roughcast and empty.

Of all the promised luxury of marble, brass, aluminium, mahogany, carpeting, curtaining and crystal, some traces are to be met with only on the lowest levels of the "Carnation", thinning out as you ascend until they reach vanishing point. In the top apartments and attics which survived decapitation (and tenantless for lack of claimants) there isn't even light or water, the walls haven't seen a touch of plaster, the floors are part bare concrete, part covered with strips of black plastic. Fifty metres below such sublimities as these the semi-basement comprises garages, storerooms, boiler-rooms and so on, for the most part unusable; but no inhabited quarters whatsoever with the sole exception of the privy cell or sentry box which has been bestowed on me and where my sublimated suicide contentedly runs its course. My duties are light enough, though to Mundula I make them out to be onerous. He laughs in my face on such occasions, but without ill-feeling, especially when I saddle myself with some trouble of his, which is fairly likely to happen, he being a pretty negligent administrator and spokesman on behalf of the distant boss; the type who waits for plenary assemblies of the tenants to become flesh in the shape of a corpulent and irritable Holy Ghost. For the rest he keeps fairly clear of the theatre of war, letting nothing escape through the unclosed doors of his office but a voice on the telephone, harsh, mournful and gruff with tobacco-smoke (goodness how he smokes!), and escaping thence only to perform some sudden spot-check, moving in the manner of a sleuth or a spy. He is held in particular terror by the charwomen, who can feel his oppressive breath on their necks before they even see him. As for myself, who have closer dealings with him because of my job, I have already had occasion to tell you that he trusts me; and in fact goes out of his way to show confidence and even curiosity in my regard. So much so that he calls me in two or three times a month for no better reason than the pleasure of conversation, of questioning me about my past as a freelance newspaperman and what gratifications it provided: evenings at the opera, interviews with the VIPs of politics and showbiz, a free ticket to the law courts, seated only a few yards from the most distinguished crooks, and so on.

Being older than me, he quotes me the case of the lady of Correggio who boiled down human bodies into soap, or else the Montesi case, and is disappointed to find me ignorant on these subjects. On the other hand, when I see an opening I pay him back by telling tall stories for all I'm worth.

Sundays, when he leaves me in peace, I spend cutting myself out a few intimate distractions. The first is to take a census of the passers-by as seen through my usual spyhole, with certain additional stratagems, such as noting the sex, probable age, style and special features of the footwear, with a view to making a statistical survey for the anthropo-socio-ethno-economic accuracy of which I would not risk a hair of my head. One example must suffice. Sunday May 14, midday till 2 a.m.: shoes, men's 71 pairs, thus divided: classic lace-ups 16, moccasins 27, espadrilles 3, flapping soles, pauperish 2, peasant clogs 1, galoshes 1, etc.; while shoes, women's, 94, of which of classic type 7, strapped sandals 3, pumps 8, slippers 4, low-cut 12, etc. This is just a sample, taking pot luck as it were, and it may be a tasty sample but – to return to my constant refrain – so what?

Another pastime, of the brain-twisting type, is making up palindromes (this very book is just one of them) or solving such puzzles as are offered me by the little mags that offer nothing else. With these I wage a life-and-death struggle induced by the ludicrous foreboding that upon this may hang the very future of a person, I don't know whom, I don't know where or how, but that person may even be me. As good a way as any other to give the game a smattering, not to say a frisson, of deadly risk.

More sedative are the hours I devote to my hoary old effort to translate Valéry's *Cimetière marin*, a Penelope's loom that I weave and unweave with tireless delight, working dogged hours at a stretch on variants of a single line without bringing myself to reject even one of them:

> Sea who know'st not thou art both one and many . . .
> Sea, who are never weary of rebirth . . .
> You who forever renew yourself, O sea . . .
> You who come back to life at every instant . . .
> O sea, a fresh beginning at every moment . . .
> You, O sea, unwearyingly renewed . . .
> You who revirginate in every wavelet . . .
> O sea, perpetual motion, endless beginning . . .
> O sea, eternal source, eternal estuary . . .
> O sea, unending pullulating heartbeat . . .
> La mer, la mer, toujours recommencée . . .

which is the ironical obvious solution I usually end up with, leaving the line as pure and perfect as your man wrote it.

I am racking my brains about this, on this particular Sunday in August, naked on the bed with a notebook in one hand and a biro in the other, when certain shrieks and tramplings of feet, of which I hear but the faintest echo, inform me that somewhere there aloft something in the mechanism of our community has slipped a cog and requires my services.

I pull on some underpants and a pair of trousers, reach the stairs and hasten up them towards what seems to be the source of the uproar. Enough to enter the main corridor, onto which open five or six apartments, to discover damsels and gentle swains in the most heterogeneous states of undress weaving this way and that – hard to say whether in a manner fortuitous or pre-established – and each one armed with some inappropriate weapon, a broom, a billiard cue, a poker . . . To cut a long story short, they are looking for a mouse.

The common house mouse, *Mus musculus*, is a greedy and prolific animal, the guest least to be desired in a dwelling of collective and decorous affluence. Euphemisms apart, a slap in the face for the honour of the building. And even then as long as it is a mouse, and not – worse sacrilege indeed – a rat up from the cellars or the sewers. No one I ask can tell me much about it. The discovery seems due to Signora Garaffa who, on rising from her bed and cautiously lowering to the floor her right footsole, which is afflicted with a painful corn, felt the sudden movement beneath it of something at the same time solid and slippery, so that she ran the risk of overbalancing and tumbling to the ground. At the same time a greyish streak crossed the room and vanished. Where? How? The door, although merely pushed to, did not provide a gap wide enough for escape. Nor did the engineer, her husband, who was in the shower and summoned by loud cries from his consort, succeed in finding any traces of the intruder other than a faint odour of wild things and a pinch or so of droppings. Explored inch by inch, the flat revealed no giveaway openings, there was nothing for it but to seek elsewhere for the enemy and its lurking-place. Hence the alarum, the unanimous dash to the scene, the breathless search. Though some harbour a suspicion, viz., that Rosalba Garaffa, eccentric enough in the mornings and woolly-headed all day long, might have been visited by one of her typical fantasies, all the more so because she (a devotee of horror movies) insists on repeating that it was not a household rodent that appeared before her, but a more horrid monster, halfway between a wingless bat and a weasel, and in either case, alas, with an almost human face.

As soon as I appear on the scene the engineer, wearing carpet slippers and a towel round his loins, though with his few remaining hairs still dripping, starts laying the blame on the guardians of condominial peace (Mundula and, in second place, myself) and threatens all hell at the next tenants' meeting. Then he suddenly darts back to his lair. He is shortly imitated by all the rest of them, and I am left alone with a young scallywag armed with a catapult. This is Maurizio, son of a separated couple by the name of Della Monica, assigned to each parent alternately for six months at a time and now doing his stint here in the care of his mother, Adriana the fortune-teller. "I saw the mouse," he boasts. "It hid behind the radiator." Behind the radiator? He must be dreaming. The thing is a good twenty centimetres clear of the floor and the intervening space is quite unencumbered; the same applies to the cavity between radiator and wall, which in any case a mouse could scale only in complete rock-climbing kit. I frown upon the lad, and he meets my look with perfect composure. But it's clear enough he's making mischief and wants an accomplice. "It's there, it's there!" he cries, pointing to an almost laughable little crack half hidden by the pink-tiled wainscot.

I decide to go along with him. I kneel down and peer intently. A funnel-shaped opening or conduit there certainly is, but of such narrowness that it could offer no possible refuge. Besides which, poking about inside with the tip of a twig, I obtain nothing but crumbs of plaster and chips of dry cement. I shrug: "Are you sure you saw something?" I ask, in total disbelief. He laughs, swivels on his heel and saunters off.

Alone at last, I am about to return to the ebb and flow of my habitual inner sea, when across the T-junction at the end of the corridor there scampers a sort of woolly something that nicks the horizon of my eyesight. I make a dash for it, but to no avail.

A mouse in flesh and blood, I begin to ask myself, or else a phantom mouse? Now I'm no great believer in ghosts, but for a moment I get a kick out of kidding myself with the thought that this gone-to-earth quarry, this evanescent lair-dweller, is in some way a metaphor of a certain Tommaso Mulè, anchorite in this world of men, over whose head is brandished just such a stick, or poker, or celestial bludgeon that one day sooner or later will beat him to pulp.

With slow steps I regain my own quarters. My notepad is still lying open on the bed. I stretch out and do my best to regain the previous ebb and flow, but I get the feeling that the sea is bestrewn with a hecatomb of slaughtered rats.

I stare at the ceiling and ruminate on my projected works. Fantastic would be a book composed entirely of titles or of first lines, a potpourri of tiny slivers, an anthology of the dramatic, comic and emotional inventions of mankind, of his myths and his frenzies . . . Or else I fall in love with the idea of the diary of one day in my life, twenty-four hours of gestures, thoughts or the embryos of thoughts, all transcribed in the most meticulous detail. Or yet again I wallow in the hypothesis of a novel which, once the opening note has been struck upon, proceeds ineluctably of its own accord, as a symphony is born from (let us say) middle C, or a rose blooms from a bud.

Needless to say it is with a memory that I intend to start: "I once purposely pricked my finger with a needle so as to be able to suck it like a nipple . . . "

Stop! That is a real memory but it sounds like a hoax. Let us look for another, false but plausible. "I am a sick man, I am an evil man. I am not an attractive man. I think my liver is playing me up. In any case I know nothing about my illness and I do not know for certain what it is that ails me . . . " Pretty good, eh? Do I see you wrinkling your noses? Ha ha, you've fallen for it!

I copied that word for word from a famous Russian whom I know by heart. Don't tell me you already knew it. And never mind if you did, I'll set you more sophisticated traps here and there, out of sheer desperation. I am a master of traps and snares.

But of that some other time. For the moment rest content with a simpler opening line: "When I was a lad I loved the sound of the rain . . . "


I am woken by a rustling sound. No, it doesn't come from the pavement up there, of which I perceive a sun-drenched but deserted strip, deserted because it is siesta time and the crush of traffic has thinned out. I am long since accustomed to the music of the wheels, whereas the sound I now hear is in this very room, though it is hard to make out exactly where it comes from. Flat on my back on the bed I try to attain a sense of direction, to give my body and its incomparable, its unique position among created things the authority and accuracy of a compass: North, South, East and West, no less than these cardinal points do I need to convince myself that I exist. The rustling comes again. A flexuous rustling if I may so put it. The sound of a flowing motion, cautious though swift, more that of a snake than of a mouse. However that may be, I persist in ignoring it and return to thoughts of myself as the axis and centre of the world, the lord and master of the wind rose. And thinking of the sun's course across the sky I calculate that I sleep with my head pointing north, reproducing in miniature the way the Italian peninsula lies in the atlas. My feet are Sicily, my left arm plunges into the Tyrrhenian, my left searches the Venetian Lagoon for the signet ring of some ancient Doge . . . But how many times over have I slept in such a privileged position? I rummage my memory for how I slept of old in barrack-room bunks, railway couchettes or rooms in hotels or pensions, double or single. What a pity

I paid no attention at the time. I have an obscure feeling that it would be enormously important for me to know which way my bed faced at La Rocca in the year X, or the one in Lugano in the year Y, or that other where I was cabin'd, crib'd, confined at the "Health and Peace" clinic in the year Z . . .

Among these weighty thoughts I fall asleep again, and this time in good earnest, without a break from the afternoon till late into the night. To the accompaniment of a strange film which unreels before my eyes as on a screen divided in two by a black line. The protagonists are: on the right a small boy, on the left a wall; and the double film narrates in parallel their birth, growth and death. On the left I watch the stones being laid, the builders at work with their trapezoid paper hats on. I scent the stench of sweat and lime. On the other side are the cries and pangs of birth and little by little the first syllables, the first laugh, the kindergarten, the school desks. When the black line gradually fades the two scenes merge into one. The wall is now covered with scribbles and graffiti, wherever there is an available gap in the bougainvillaea, and the boy is practising goalkicks against it, and I hear the smack of ball against wall like the rhythmical taps of a mallet. Two kindred stories then, equal and opposite, the one that of an inert *res extensa*, as they taught me to say at school, and the other as warm with life, hectic with action, laughing and crying and even thinking (for what that's worth) . . .

That the child was me in the dream is dead certain, just as it was that as a grown-up I was spectator, judge and justicer of that embryo of myself. The very same who goes on bashing, at first with footballs but thereafter with his fists, at that gimcrack wall, and particularly the bottom of it, where a fissure concealed by the climbing plants has been growing ever wider. Until, after an even mightier blow, with a crash like the dropping of crockery, the wall crumbles to dust, covers the body of the pugnacious boy and smothers him in a small but catastrophic shambles. All you can see protruding from the rubble is a single hand, that seems to twitch and beg for help, and between one brick and another there's the sliver of a face, a temple grazed as red as raw meat. This pierces the screen of my dream and wakes me up.

I decide not to look into all that for any explanation or premonition or what you will. Ever since I realized that my dreams are nearly always self-slanders or spiteful gossip at my own expense, I don't pay them much attention, I simply brush them aside. And yet this latest one, with its masked and menacing folly of unreason, leaves a lump in my throat, not so much of anxiety as of irritation. Heavy with sleep, I cannot pluck up courage to open my eyes. It must be three or four in the morning, still the dead of night, the jar where I live still full of jammy blackness. In which, all of a sudden, I hear a little squeak, as small as can be, almost a whimper. At first I ignore it, it's centuries now that I've been living with the noises of the night without attempting to make them out, convinced that they are a coded language into which it would be indiscreet to poke my nose. But as it goes on and on, and sounds all too much like the voice of a small animal we all know well, with a swift silent movement I flick on the light and take a look around. For such a small bare room one glance is enough. The chest of drawers where I keep my clothing sits as snugly as ever against the long wall on the street side of the room, as square, smooth and inexpressive as a block of ice; on the table which flanks and overtops it are the customary objects: an old steel paper-knife stamped "Butera & Merini", a portable radio, a bronze inkpot (empty), the professional model Olivetti typewriter, my dictionaries and the seven books that compose my library, my surviving Seven Against Thebes, ill-assorted kings of an army of ashes . . . Nothing, in short, that resembles a mouse or a place where a mouse might hide. And even so, I have decided to make war on him no more, and no one will make me budge from this bed before ten o'clock. I have grown too fond of this wool-gathering, the most recent discovery of my peace-loving impulses. Neither sleeping nor dreaming, but a sort of escapist fiction that when I shut my eyes I conjure up as the mood takes me, blending daydreams of my own with scraps from the classics into a huge ragout of compatible images, to guard against the drab agenda that faces me tomorrow. "I am mute, therefore I daydream." Nor for this purpose do I need darkness, but on the contrary the aid of some oblique, extenuated light, for example a neon sign or the swivelling headlights of passing cars that reach to me through my peephole, which until this moment I have muted with the curtains.

But now I let them in, manipulating the long rod I keep by me to remove the screen without leaving my bed. The same thing tonight, or even better, for tonight in addition there is a moon. It is not the dazzle of cars or of street-lamps, but herself in person who, in a manner known only to her, from that sliver of sky where she is pinned between chimneypot and rooftop, pours in her porcelain-pure luminescence even until it alights upon my pillow. A real moon or a dummy-moon, I ask myself, picking up on the recent string of reproaches so dear to my blind friend. Not long ago he accused me of living a dummy-life, and tonight I am inclined to say him yea. For when it comes to the moon I realize that in me, in the sheer dreariness of my mere survival, all inner fire is forgotten; in this paralysis of feeling in which the passions of yore leave only the faintest of scars, one wound still smarts; and it is, I blush to confess, infatuation with the moon.

Myriads of moons did I relish in times past. And I muddle up those I really experienced with those I only read about. I no longer know whether it was in a book or during some real calendar summer that I lifted up my arms towards a cloud, waiting for a ray of hers to pierce it and drench me in her light; I no longer know whether it was one real calendar summer, or else in some book, that I went floating forth in an oarless boat, a rocking-chair of languorous light, trailing my hands in the water till they drowned in liquid pearl, but only to rise up again as the whitest of flowers, dripping with gems . . .

But part of my own real life, no doubt about it, was that night when I walked the overgrown old railway tracks between Ginisi and Donnafugata, and an old song rose to my lips: "Milk-white pathway sprinkled with silver" . . . Whereas less weepy is the memory of certain pages I read in my youth (could it be *Le rêve*?): a multitude of stars in the sky, a lake unimaginably sparkling glimpsed between stacks of timber as tall as the pyramids, amongst which two young people in love went hand in hand. Moon-struck birds of youth, shall I ever be free of you?

But day is upon us here. Again the inevitable thunder of tyres over the humps in the asphalt. But I dig deeper down into my lethargy, I don't even respond to the metallic rapping with which at about nine o'clock Tiresias asks if I want to see him. He makes no reply to my silence, and I listen to his halting steps growing fainter and fainter.

And the mouse? It has crept into my head through a lughole while I was sleeping. You cannot imagine what minuteness those creatures can shrink to, when you are dreaming them.

# FOUR

# Round the Houses

*Thursday, August 17th*

Amongst the seeds of discord that inflame the bosoms of the citizens of Flower City – such as being rained on by flowerpots from the floor above; leaving the lift door open out of sheer carelessness (or perhaps on purpose, to prevent anyone else pinching it), and the everlasting warfare over carpet-beating and laundry on the line – one of the most envenomed of all is the choice of the place and time in which to hold our periodical tenants' meetings. If we can reach agreement on a date and time of day it already seems a miracle, though every so often it comes off. It is on the *venue* of the meeting that any consensus becomes impossible, because no lady of the house would, even over her dead body, permit the smokers' smoke to infest her home or allow unhallowed feet to trample her polished floors. Beaten down on my idea of taking it by turns, or by lottery, Mundula's over-riding decision is that we shall meet on the first Sunday in September in a large empty apartment on the top floor, in the vicinity of which, to make up for the utter bareness of the place, Adele has established a storeroom for chairs.

The order of the day, written in the hand of the Great Chief himself, belligerently lays it down that the meeting should decide on the following questions. 1) Can we continue to tolerate the presence in the apartments of domestic animals, such as dogs,

cats, hamsters, parrots and so on? 2) Is it worth accepting the
exorbitant contractual terms insisted on by the lift-maintenance
firm? 3) Can the tenants tolerate the way the trumpeter Biscelgie,
who lives on the sixth floor and is way in arrears with his
rent, plays his jazz numbers night and day with earth-shattering
effects rating high on the Richter scale? 4) Is it compatible with
proper moral conduct that Mr Torquato Marino, known profes-
sionally as "Mariposa", should flaunt his female wardrobe both
inside the building and elsewhere, as we have been informed
by persons who have witnessed him plying his trade in the most
conspicuous transvestite haunts? 5) Any other business.

It falls to my lot, as ever, to call on all the persons concerned,
coax them into signing the form, and ask them to be there on
time. What a tedious *via crucis* it would be, were it not that, albeit
fleetingly, it gives me certain succulent glimpses of what goes
on inside, as in one of the occupations I envy most, that of
the door-to-door encyclopaedia salesman. The reader will not
be at a loss to understand that I, having confined myself to a
very limited, immutable living space, remote from the endless
surprises that life has to offer, am inclined to compensate for
this loss by finding an outlet in gossipy curiosity, just as in any
secluded society: seminaries, cloisters, small town squares . . .
Therefore, like a janitor with not much work on his hands, I not
only count and collect the legs of passers-by, but amuse myself
whenever possible by snatching at the more or less innocuous
secrets of my companions in destiny.

This explains why my first visit is to the residence of the printer
Malatesta Buozzi and his daughter Leah, recent recruits to our
ranks and now installed on the first floor. From what one gathers
he is an anarchist resigned to bourgeois existence, but disagree-
able to all and sundry, as everyone is to him, if we are to judge
from his abrupt and touchy mode of speech, and a scowl that

seems an angry reproach to the universe at large. She, whom we have already admired in her doorway on the day of the mouse-hunt, holding up the hem of her dressing-gown lest the hunted creature should seek refuge therein and start climbing . . . A gown the colour of dark claret, from which there soared a neck and a visage of ivory whiteness. What an eburnean statue, I thought, except for the eyes: incredulous, astonished, thrilled at first by this unusual adventure; thereafter, released from apprehension, two blue lakes touched by a last roseate dazzle, as when with a twig you stir the ashes of a dying fire. A fiery lass but timid, in a word, whom the presence of her parent reduced to silence (I have never heard her utter a word).

It is in fact Buozzi who opens the door, listens to what I have to say and brusquely sends me packing, clumsily interposing his body between me and the girl, who is over by the window sewing and scarcely raises her eyes from her hemstitching. Silent again – I must really make an effort to discover her voice.

And at this point I think I must put in a word to the effect that in this peaceful isolation of mine I have not ceased to think of women. I say to think, no more than that. For my physical requirements are met by my intermittent effusions with one or other of the charwomen. Whereas the Idea of women, the pure thought, is an arduous and tender art which I cultivate with all the scrupulousness of a seminarian. Nothing that leads to actually doing anything, but only an endless bird's-eye-view of the approaches to love; or else, in more modern terms, trial runs for the love-race. With a purely imagined gusto of pleasure in which I enswathe a body and a face in a fairy-tale cocoon, in a randy-chaste orgy of gestures, words and swoons; in which all the emotions of a lifetime come together and achieve the fusion of innumerable effigies into one as unique and superb as she is estranged from me. A mélange of Natasha Filipovna, Louise

Brooks, La Belle Cordière, plus that sixteen-year-old I caught a glimpse of in 1971 on the ferry to Elba . . .

Thus between them and me, between *her* and me, there is a mass of possibilities, all predictable, as in a game of patience when you've rigged the cards from the start.

(Rosa? Ah yes, her too, and why not? If only for the sake of that night of gentle rain, when we walked barefoot in the park, having just seen *Singin' in the Rain*.)

On the next floor up – whereto the lift hoists me with a wheeze like a worn-out windlass – lives Gregorio Crisafulli, who opens the door to me already laughing.

An eccentric in from the country, not a city man, is Gregorio. In his heyday the manager of a touring company of players and fluctuating fortunes; not without some histrionic prowess, evinced mainly by the texts he has written himself, roundly booed in every theatre throughout the neighbourhood, now reduced by length of days and hardening of the arteries to a dignified (he claims disdainful) life as a pensioner. Much loved by us for his manic whimsicalities and his outbursts both verbal and mental, to such an extent that we bite the bullet and pretend to be an audience not only won over but overwhelmed, whenever there's a tenant's meeting or a day of really foul weather, and he asks to give us one of his one-act jobs performed by solo voice and a cast of cardboard silhouettes.

I should make myself clearer. In the loft where we are due to meet he has taken it into his head to set up a stage of sorts, and when due occasion brings us all there, he alone, acting out all the parts in their various voices, as puppeteers with their puppets, does not fail to wheedle and threaten us into attention. For the secondary roles he avails himself of carnival masks and the pickings from fancy-dress parties which he buys off the market

stalls at Porta Portese and arranges against a wall to make a dumb
show to back up his rigmaroles. From time to time throwing
them a catchword and receiving some wisecrack in return, all of
which invariably issue, of course, from his own thespian lips. That
there's a touch of dottiness in all this is the majority opinion, but
we're willing to muck in, and even contribute, each according to
his means, to buying the cardboard silhouettes, and if occasion
arises even come on stage to do our best as sidekicks.

"Have you seen the latest?" he eagerly enquires from the
doorway before drawing me inside and pointing to a corner
containing a life-size figure of a tall-hatted chef giving you the
come-hither with a dish of spaghetti, such as one sees along
the roadside in tourist spots. I have no idea how Gregorio came
by it, but knowing that he has lately returned from an excursion
for elderly and disabled persons, financed by the Council, I'll lay
my oath that it is the swag from some nocturnal foray.

To persuade him to sign is an absolute snip. He'd do it ten
times over to get us all together there, his minions after the
meeting, spectators of his latest efforts, which he hastens to tell
me are called *The Filibuster*.

"You'll see, you'll see!" he tells me with his small, accomplice
eyes a-glitter. "It's top-notch stuff, you'll give me an ovation.
And then, if Mundula were to allow me a small discount on
the rent . . . After all, I contribute to the entertainment of the
community . . ."

"I'll speak to him about it, put in a word for you," I assure him
in complete bad faith and make my escape.

Continuing my tour, and leaving out the many tenants who
are too insignificant to find a place in my narrative, here I am
standing before Tir's door. We haven't seen one another, if one
may use the reciprocal plural in speaking of a blind man, since

our last foray into the streets. I give our usual signal, three knocks with a pause between the second and the third, but no one answers. I try the door, and it opens. I grope my way into the dark room, feel for the light-switch. The bedroom door is shut, so I open it. Bartolomeo, fully dressed and awake, is stretched out on the bed. No sign of Matilde or of Cesare.

"Tommaso," he says weakly, having recognized me by my knock, "leave me alone." Then, in a sudden change of mood: "Take me outside, I want to photograph the sun." He doesn't wait for me to say no, he has already turned on his side with his face to the wall. I sit beside him, and talk gently to his heaving shoulders: "Tir," I say, "they'll come back. Where do you imagine they could go?"

I take it for granted that he has already tumbled to the meaning of the double disappearance of the boy and his sister. Not only that, but I strongly suspect that he already knew it, and that the photo I charitably hid from him would probably have come as no surprise.

From the way he is clenching his fists I imagine he is suffering. And I have a surge of ridiculous rage as I think of all the millions and millions of men in the world who at this very moment are tormenting themselves with suchlike fatuities of sorrow: vortices, occlusions, clots, traps, tangles of sentiment, short-lived and constantly erased by time as the wind every instant changes the face of the sea. "The sea, the sea . . . " I grumble between clenched teeth and leave him moaning there. "I'll come back later," I tell him. "We'll go and photograph the sun."

The next lap would take in the Garaffas, man and wife, so many of the others being scattered for the holidays over various beaches and mountain resorts. Garaffa, however, I find outside in the corridor talking quietly to a builder. This latter is wearing the classic uniform of his job, almost as if personifying it in a parade of the arts and crafts: blue shirt blotched with whitewash, rag-wrapped boots, red pencil stuck behind his ear. I observe him with some astonishment, for beneath the vigilant scrutiny of the Engineer Garaffa he is fussing away at a crack in the wall, an almost invisible fissure that runs from floor to ceiling. The workman, with freckled hands covered with reddish hair, is sticking bits of tape across the cracks. I ask why. "To keep the crack under surveillance," replies Garaffa. "They do the same thing on the Leaning Tower of Pisa. If the tape snaps it means that the structure is moving and you have to watch it."

Here the workman puts in a word: "It's a matter of what we call ground settling," he stated authoritatively. "It's a perfectly normal phenomenon with new constructions."

I take his word for it. Though this Garaffa is a man of imperceptible intelligence, and it would be odd if he weren't a complete dolt in engineering as well . . .

Getting him off my back still leaves me most of them to do, concentrated on the upper floors. Starting on the sixth, where dwells the trumpet player threatened with eviction. Not only because he's months in arrears with the rent, but because he lets it rip too loudly on his instrument. I have to say I don't mind this, partly because down where I live the noise arrives muffled by several storeys, and partly because I love the stuff he plays, especially the one that goes didi-dee didi-dahdi di-deee, and goes by the name of the St James Infirmary Blues.

Johnny signs very unwillingly. "Do I really have to come?" he asks gloomily.

Blondish, youngish, he did his utmost to resemble his idol, whose name I believe was Bix. Only a silk scarf round his neck and a waistcoat of many colours survive from the dandy air he probably affected when, as he claims, he was a star attraction from midnight until five in the morning in a hot spot at Gatteo-on-Sea.

"Care for a whisky?" says he.

"No, it's bad for me."

"Anybody's whisky, or just mine?" he comes back at me with a quip that smacks to me of the movies.

"Yours or anybody else's," I snap back. But he moans on, "Do I really have to come? What'll happen if I don't?"

I manage to persuade him that he is the only one who can conceivably plead his cause, that a friendly agreement is always possible. He must pay up, of course, Mundula won't hear a word of objection on that score, but there are ways and means. Maybe a deferment, maybe an instalment plan.

Having got over that one I'm back in the corridor again. Here I come upon the two young Greek twins, George and Constantine Argiropoulos, with whom the lad Maurizio plays a cruel game. As they live in next-door apartments, the three of them were bound to be thrown together. The fact is that Maurizio bullies them mercilessly, imposing impossible forfeits on them when – by cheating – he has beaten them at cards. Such as making them race on all fours, one from each end of the corridor, to the point in the middle where he is waiting to force the loser to lick his shoes. The docility of both the twins towards their persecutor is out of this world. As far as I know, their parents, Katina and Demetrios, who import oriental carpets, have no idea how things really stand, though feeling a vague anxiety, if not a threat. But whenever they have tried to break off this sinister relationship the simultaneous reaction of their sons – bursting into tears, throwing themselves on the ground, beating their fists against the wall – has quite scared them and induced them to desist, leaving the young ones to follow that inclination all the way, hoping that the obnoxiousness of the tyrant will finally drive them to rebellion or that, as they grow older, they will by nature become their own masters.

I step over them as they roll in the dust, acting out some pantomime of redskins or cannibals, and through the open doorway (left open, I imagine, by a father's solicitude as to the scene outside) I call out "Signor Demetrios". Tall, thin, gawky and foxy-eyed, he scarcely looks at the sheet of paper and scribbles his signature, not without casting a glance along the corridor, at the point where it plummets into the stairwell. The boys have vanished, we hear only the sound of their scampering feet, ever fainter. They are probably transferring their game to the cellars, if not out onto the pavements of the main road.

On I go. On the next door, just ajar, and above a tiny doll on a string – a lucky charm – the name-plate offers me but the one name only: Adriana. I push at the door and walk straight in, I know I'm allowed to. The waiting room I now enter is fairly densely populated. Adriana is a sorceress of high standing, she works with the Tarot, she reads your hand, and can infallibly cure the pangs of love as well as pains in the back. The six people waiting all have a look of faith and misgiving, or hanging halfway between the two, I think, and there's no doubt but a favourable prophesy or a herbal potion perforce must help them . . . As has certainly happened with the client who now, radiant with exultation, emerges from the lady's consulting room and gives us "Good morning" with a fanfare and flourish of so many decibels as to make us imagine the promise of fruit to a hitherto sterile womb, or of a rich uncle in Australia dropping a fortune into the lap of a beggar.

I take the front place in the queue. As in doctors' waiting rooms purveyors of medicinal ads are sent right on in, so I am given precedence because I have so little to ask. Adriana also signs without reading the agenda. "I already know what it's about," she chuckles. "The Tarots don't lie."

This Adriana is a plump lady fairly well advanced in years. I imagine she still feels certain yearnings of the flesh, judging from the way her bosom casually brushes against the hand holding the clip-file of all the statements to be signed. "There's so many people out there," I splutter, and make off. "Come to me for a consultation from time to time," she calls after me down the corridor. "All free of charge, of course."

I take to my heels and here I am at the seventh floor, buzzing for ages and to no effect at the door of Lo Surdo. He must be off on one of his thousand fruitless trudges from one office to another in an effort to obtain money from insurance to reimburse him after the fire which some years ago destroyed his paper-mill. It was arson and no doubt about it, but whereas he maintains that it was the work of extortioners the insurance company suspects that he set fire to the place himself.

Very well, I'll come back and find him later on. As for the next visitee, Mariposa, I know that she leaves home at dusk, returns at dawn, and sleeps through until four in the afternoon. So as not to wake her I slip a note under the door, asking her to call on me before going to work. After which I have to face Pirzio Ravalli, chartered accountant, who of all of us here is the most mysterious. I have to ring for ages before he decides to open the door a crack, through which he scrutinizes me with hostile eye:

"It's for the meeting. I'll only take a moment."

He removes the chain and lets me in. I let my own critical eye rove over the residence. The furnishings and appointments betray some measure of prosperity, but the kitchen sink, glimpsed through the open folding door, is piled with dirty dishes. He himself has come to the door holding a pair of dripping socks. I scarcely know what to think. Mistrust is painted all over his every word and gesture. If it were not that the name Pirzio is too unusual to be a fake, I would suspect him of another identity as a bandit, a terrorist, a spy . . . This is partly because it seems implausible that every time he hands me his month's rent it is in brand-new 100,000-lire notes, that he carries on no visible activity whatever, but stays shut up at home (although I am scarcely one to be surprised), and that all we know of his invisible lady friend is that she is called Gioele and is out of town. I think, as I visit them, that each one of these creatures is better than I am. Almost none of them, I bet, wastes time asking themselves the questions that I constantly pester myself with, the classic "who are we? whence come we? whither are we bound?". To which I can find no answer more convincing than the one I once heard someone give: "I am me, I have come from home, I'm going back there". A fatuity as good as any other, to tame not so much yesterday's mouse (which has gone away) as a number of small hyenas that are chewing away at my brain. Sometimes, mostly at night, I hear them inside me whining with hunger and longing. That makes me feel like some sort of itinerant cage, a human zoo full of hides and claws and teeth . . . The doctor tells me it's this stuff diazine that awakens such monsters in my head. All right, but how could I invent their panting breath, their stench, if they weren't already familiar to me? However, the truth is that if I double the dose of this drug I sleep like a log and don't dream at all.

The eighth floor, immediately under the unoccupied garrets and attics, the last stage of my gymnastic itinerary. Thank God, I say to myself, that I only have to do it once a month. It's not, I repeat, that I mind nosing around among people, after such a long diet of solitude, but the pickings I obtain from it this morning, which are supposed to come in useful for the novel I am writing, are nothing but a meagre and lustreless cross section of the middle classes. With great potentialities, needless to say: very often a crime or a portent emerges from the greyest of routine.

Not, however, from apartments 31 and 32, inhabited by two old people living alone: the first is a lady of noble family fallen on hard times, Donna Marzia De Castro, the second a pensioned-off professor of philosophy, Placido Carnemolla. The first is pushing eighty, the second well into his seventies.

Regarding Donna Marzia, I must tell you that she survives by selling off what is left of the family furniture, and in particular, each year, one of the six remaining survivors of her former collection of paintings and prints: "I have bread for six years," she says. "It'll see me through, I don't mean to live longer than that." She keeps them under the bed, and only I know their value: a Piranesi, a Monsù Desiderio, a possible Beccafumi, a school of Arcimboldo (a good one), a *Malinconia* by Grechetto, a panel by Biccherna . . . I am always afraid they will be stolen, but she is unperturbed: "No one knows except you, and you I trust. And in any case I've got this." And from under a cushion she produces a huge pistol loaded with blanks. "If anyone comes I'll knock him dead just with the din of it."

She invites me in, but I decline. I know that next door I shall be held up for quite a while, Placido does not let visitors off lightly, he's one of those non-stop talkers, it must be an illness. After half an hour of it I'm on the ropes, but I have to confess that the first half-hour is a treat.

He opens the door in a bizarre costume, half winter half summer: cotton longjohns down to his ankles (with the temperature over 30°) and an impalpable singlet covering a snow-white torso unctuous with ancient sweat. Not a word of greeting, he simply continues with one of his garrulous monologues:

"The best age to fall in love is mine. Before seventy you have very confused ideas about women and love . . . "

I try and get a word in: "Please, just a quick signature."

He embraces me, seizes my clip-board, puts it down on the piano, and forces me into a chair with a gentle pressure on my shoulders: "A cup of tea? It comes from Manila. Prepared with my own hands." My refusal does nothing to discourage him. "Don't get up. What's the hurry? If you can do a thing slowly, do it more slowly still. Alas for one obliged to run when everything would have him lie down."

He is speaking of himself. Just in case I hadn't realized this, he supplied a gloss: "Like me, pursued by ferocious creditors . . . "

"Creditors? You?"

"My arrears are the years," he explains with a theatrical gesture. Then, laughing: "To be called Placido and be forced to run, just imagine!" I laugh along with him but "Listen," he goes on, "do you know what I thought this morning? I thought of the relationship between myself and me. It must be a bond as strong as steel. It is in all animals, every animal loves itself. Only man has discovered that it is more natural not to love oneself than to love oneself . . . "

The notion takes my fancy, I open my ears.

"I despise myself," he continues, "and I am seeking for allies. Wouldn't you care to despise me just a little? It would be a friendly gesture."

"Despise you? I wouldn't dare."

"A firm dislike," he proclaims solemnly, "is the best basis for a friendship."

"You're too high in the clouds for me. Please explain."

"Forgive me, but the truth is always intricate. Have you ever watched Americans struggling to eat spaghetti? So it is with us and the truth."

I don't take offence, I know he thinks well of me. "Very well,"

I beg him with a smile, "lower yourself to the level of my humble cellar."

He assumes an air of grave learning but at the same time gives me a wink: "Open up, I'll be right there. Let us begin with an incontrovertible fact: the grandeur and sanctity of old age. In Fascist times a Socialist grandfather of mine, whenever they forced him to sing *"Giovinezza"*, used to run straight home and re-read the *De senectute*. What do I mean by this? That an old man is a fine thing, like an old tree: he has roots, and memory, and the sublime awareness of death close at hand. Also he is younger than a young man, especially if when young he was able to be old. This is not a play on words: we need to have been very old when young, to be able to be young when old. The only trouble is . . . "

Despite my good intentions I am finding this pretty hard going. But he charges on: "The only trouble is that it's no fun being rich when the others aren't poor. In other words it grieves me that there are other old men as well as me. I would wish to be the only one to remember the voice of Zarah Leander or Carlos Gardel on those curfewed evenings during the war. But instead there are still lots of us, I'm jealous of the memories of the rest of them . . . "

"But what's this got to do," I protested, "with loving oneself or otherwise?"

"Plenty," said he. "How can we possibly love ourselves when we live with ourselves twenty-four hours a day? It's easier to love our neighbour, of whom we see only an anthology of the best bits. It's therefore legitimate, and I would say inevitable, for me to find myself hard to bear. On the other hand there's a whole wealth of memories, dawns and moons and faces innumerable, and all this, how could I fail to love it? This is the reason for the breach in me: I love the old man that is in me,

I detest the young man I still feel myself to be . . . ”

He got into a muddle, he seemed all of a sudden wounded and pitiful and defenceless. I laid a hand on his arm.

“Youth,” he mumbled, “there's always something faintly ridiculous about it. All the same, how I wish, how I wish . . . ”

He broke off, burst into tears, burst out laughing, and literally, though playfully, kicked me out.

On the watch in my usual catacomb, waiting for the white shoes and nut-brown trousers of Enrico Lo Surdo to appear within range of my private porthole. He has no choice but to pass me, if he wants to get to the entrance, nor does the waiting worry me, it's part of my usual game. All the better since I get a second bird with the same stone. This is Mariposa who at dusk, after a good sleep, is just off to work. I let out a bawl recognizable as mine, for she knows that hatchway beside the main door is my telescope trained on the world, and when she passes she seldom fails to say something. “Wait,” I roar at her, “wait!” and I bound out and join her.

She twists my note this way and that in her fingers, and asks: “I had decided not to come. Won't it embarrass people?” Though she at once adds: “I don't receive at home, I give no cause for scandal.”

“You come,” I insist, “and stick up for yourself tooth and nail. I'm on your side.”

She signs slowly with a lipstick, ignoring my proffered pen; then, teetering on her high heels, off she goes.

Barely half an hour later and here is Lo Surdo. I catch him in the hall on the brink of flight, but block him at the door of the lift.

“Get in,” he says, with a scowl on a Mediterranean face baked as brown as a terracotta pot. His eyes are wild, his speech impetuous and frantic, he is looking for someone to take it out on.

I hold out the clip-board. "A tenants' meeting, who gives a damn?" he laughs bitterly. All the same he signs the agenda without reading it, standing there in the lift which has already started upwards. He has no time to give it me back before the light goes out, the cage jolts to a stop, total blackout.

We curse in unison, then both grope for the alarm button, in case some merciful soul should hear us and, by use of the hand mechanism, deliver us from these two cubic metres of air, hanging lifeless. But just imagine if a mere bell can compete with the strident blare of Johnny Bisceglie's solos. To make things worse he loves to play in the dark, a power cut is manna in the desert for him, so God knows when he'll shut up.

So then Lo Surdo starts to talk. I get the impression that he is repeating the defence he just now put up for himself before the untrusting tricksters of the insurance claims department. Maybe he's having another go, in the hope of persuading me at least.

He says . . . But how can I possibly pay attention, trapped as I am in a panic of being buried alive in a stood-on-end bier in a stony well-shaft with the echo of a distant trumpet in my ear? He rattles hectically on, but all I want is to get out into the open, I'm suffocating in here. Thank God that the very moment he ends his tale the light is restored, the lift jerks into motion again. A coincidence that works in his favour, because without having gathered more than a few scraps of his side of the matter, from sheer joy I hasten to bid him good evening, and after a vigorous handshake take my leave.

# FIVE

# In Actual Fact

*Tuesday, August 22nd*

What a wind tonight! Whence did it come, from what unknown borderlands? I can't stand its whimpering and wailing, that subdued ubiquitous mooing . . . If I could translate it into human terms I'm sure it would reveal but some airy gossip, some harmless mystery. But in the tricks of its twists and turns I cannot help feeling some evil intention; and hearing in its voice, as at a time of prophetic sleepless nights, a death-knell tolling for the August that is dying. It's just as well that autumn is still to come, indeed its forward outposts are already through the mountain passes and are scaring the topmost weathercocks of the city. Only this moment I heard distant thunder strike a gong-like note, as if by way of challenge. Oppressed at heart, and staring into the darkness, in vain I try the light-switch every five minutes. The power has failed yet again, and if I want to know the time I have to peer at the alarm clock by the light of a candle.

Would that a morsel of light filtered in through the curtains, that a conspicuous draught opens and closes like an eyelid! But nothing is remotely perceptible, not even the usual pallid gleam of the streetlights, the power cut has cut them too. If I imagine a hand that cleaves through the thick of the darkness, it is only a phantom hand; if I hope for a vision to make me weep blood, it is only the phantom face of God. Yes, this I do imagine and hope for: that on that shroud, that curtain, a face will one day be stamped, perhaps even the face of a scoundrel, one of the many disguises of the Great Conjuror. And that, without believing in him, is how I picture God: a fancy-dress Fra Diavolo, with a black patch over one eye. Or else our philosopher Placido has the right answer: God is a fish that swims in deep waters, and divers pass close by him without seeing him, but tomorrow or the next day he will come to the surface, we shall see him darting in the water of our wells, of our swimming pools.

But I was speaking of the wind . . . Which in my fantasy tonight impersonates a whistle of warning sent out by the great spaces and the stars, the shrill creaking of the axis of the world. To tell the whole truth and nothing but the truth, I never for a moment forget that I live on a crumb of rock spinning like a top and surrounded by the incommensurable void . . . In my own insignificant portion of earth I move as if walking on eggshells, to the point of being scared lest my footing slip from under me, break apart, swallow me up. Under my shoes I feel the earth not a whit more solid than the surface of the sea.

I once mentioned this to Placido: "A very Pascalian awareness of the abyss," he observed with his nose in the air. "But even more, these things are in your blood because you were born in a part of the world they call 'ballerina', because it dances about under your feet." And he would have gone on, but I made my escape: I had an appointment with Mundula for the monthly accounting.

From this I return, as ever, laden with rebukes for getting the sum wrong, or muddling up the names. It has by now become so likely for me to muddle up names and figures that every time it's touch-and-go whenever I'm forced to extricate them exactly from the porridge of calculations that fouls up my mind. I am short on method, on orderliness. If for no other reason I'll devote a page of this notepad where I am jotting down fantasies and reminiscences to the life histories of the various characters of whom I have spoken and will continue to speak.

A list in alphabetical order, starting with the two Argiropuloi and ending with Pirzio Ravalli, and sandwiched between them Mariposa and Bisceglie and the dumb-cluck Garaffas, and the distressed noblewoman De Castro, and Buozzi the printer, and myself – urban speleologist – and Bartolomeo Guelfi, known as Tir, suppliant for the light of day and pathetic mal-aimé . . .

At a rough guess, barring the two dumb-clucks, we are a bunch of unhappy people. No one here seems to have reason for contentment, from the sorceress Adriana, afflicted with an untrustworthy son and a flabby belly, to the philosopher Carnemolla, who is scared of death and of the passing of time. Another bond between us is the reluctance, whether by choice or necessity, to go away on holiday, our attachment to this condominial Bastille, this stuccoed tower of third-rate cement, as permeable to heat as a belly to a stiletto.

So what fun it will be next Sunday, all together with our gibes, our mutual reproaches, tantrums, feeble jokes, the smell of sweaty armpits . . . With our good lawyer Mundula at the head of the table, poor devil: he has thrice failed his exams to become a solicitor and is reduced to acting as spokesman and cashier to his transatlantic cousin. An unhappy bunch, I repeat, but one of us is more unhappy than the rest. I refer to Enrico Lo Surdo, if I am to believe in his "actual fact" (thus, somewhat tautologically, does he define any event the truth of which he wishes to affirm with emphasis). Of this I know certain scraps, gathered from his own lips in the lift the day before yesterday or whimpered by his wife later on when I met her on the landing. That they are the truth and nothing but the truth I wouldn't be prepared to swear. However, they are what is wanted in a story with

social atmosphere, such as suits the Monthly Supplement of the
"Spyglass". With a few additions and stylistic trappings I could
turn them into a marketable article and send it to the paper,
should I ever again became a contributor . . .

Here are the first few pages. The rest comes later.

### Serious Narrative – Part One

*The scene is laid in Sicily in the region of "Blank" (Lo Surdo won't let
on about it), one Friday evening in front of his paper-mill. There he is
after working hours, with two of his employees, gazing at the empty,
silent factory reposing in the warmth of the sunset. It is the hour when
it is no longer day but dusk still dallies on the horizon, imbuing the
landscape with a gentle music, almost a somnolent rinsing of the air;
when every word uttered sounds as if in a dream swathed in cotton-wool.*

*Little given to the enchantments of eventide, he has a bee in his
bonnet about a fixed "Milan-Vicenza 2" on the football pools, whereas
his fellow punters turn a deaf ear to his arguments. Now that the
working week is at an end, and subordination with it, they strongly
object to their boss's prophetic pretensions. At that instant the telephone
rings, scarcely audible from the forecourt-cum-parking lot where
the three of them are standing. Lo Surdo goes back into the factory
through the still-unshuttered goods entrance, traverses the ground-floor
warehouse, a lean-to with lots of metal gratings and piled high with
bales of rags which the forklift-truck unloaded from the lorry that
afternoon, and climbs slowly (let them ring, there's no hurry) to the
mezzanine, used for the beating and cleansing of the fibres. He proceeds
at leisure with the bold, self-confident step of one to whom a telephone
might utter a plea, or a complaint, but no really bad news. He is in
good health, he has a beautiful wife, no child who might get lost or
burnt, but a solid bank account and assured solvency. Whoever this
pest is, bawling himself hoarse to get in touch with him after hours,
at the sacred hour of filling in his football-pool coupon, let him wait.*

He has reached his office. The air in the passageway is thick with rag-dust and filament. This enrages him, if he's told them once he's told them a thousand times to let fresh air into the place . . . At last he opens the door, enters, steps to the desk, picks up the receiver, cutting short the thirtieth ring: "Hullo?"

Not a word from the other end, but a solid presence, the heavy breathing of one who has run a mile or is suffering from emphysema.

"Hullo?" repeats Lo Surdo and is about to hang up, this being the third or fourth time he has been troubled by callers who vanish on the instant. Children playing games, or grown-ups a bit short of the grey-matter?

But this time the faintest whisper of a voice comes at last in answer: "Priparassi cinquanta miliuna . . . "

What! Get fifty million lire together? So even here in his own home town the Black Hand has arrived. It has happened to lots of people, but elsewhere, he never thought it would happen even here, even to him . . .

He snaps out a "No!" and hangs up. But he is far from easy in his mind as he rejoins Licausi and Tirrò, his betting-mates, there in the car park.

"All right, let's go for that 'Milan-Vicenza 2' that you were insisting on . . ."

But he isn't listening: "Have it your own way, I'll come along with you in any case. And in the meanwhile you two buzz off, I'll stay on here for a while."

And stay he does. It is now almost nightfall. The outlines of the factory are blurred, then erased by the deepening shades. A gem of a factory, such as they might hanker after even in the North. A perfect unity of stone, steel and water which, with the latest improvements, seems to him to have achieved a kind of human equilibrium, the minute perfection of a living creature, such as he himself dreamt of as a child when by screwing together pieces of Meccano he strove to build a fairy-tale castle. A perfect object, a lovesome thing. Not all that *incompatible either with his erstwhile dream of becoming a writer. Seeing that nothing was to prevent him believing that those great snow-white sheets he manufactured and sold might, even by the hand of others, be tinctured with glorious ink and immortal writings . . .*

*He had given up writing almost at once, and in his heart of hearts was glad of his decision, thinking of the thousands who painfully persevere. Enough for him to finger the reams that came forth fragrant and virgin from his machines, and to rub his nose on them with all the voracity of a ferret.*

*He turns his eyes to boundary wall. Stacked against it are the bales prepared for long haulage, and here is the parking lot, with three little three-wheeler vans like puppies alongside a gigantic truck and trailer.*

*Of all he surveys he is the monarch, he, Enrico Lo Surdo. He reigns over this little kingdom, and with it the numerous families who depend on it for their living, and the far, far more numerous railway-men, printers, authors, journalists, newsagents, librarians, booksellers, grocers, schoolchildren, who might by chance have touched, handled or used these sheets of paper and by their means scattered to the winds the truths and falsehoods of the world.*

*By no means new to such lofty thoughts, Lo Surdo for the umpteenth time renders silent thanks to his father. It was the latter's express dying wish to persuade his son to exchange a shaky academic career for this round of daily chores that has gradually come to reveal itself to be the wisest choice of his life. And from it have proceeded other happy choices: marriage to a propertied woman of a fleshy and somewhat faded beauty, but with a good head on her shoulders, the incomparable administrator of all that is his; childless as they were by choice, untroubled affluence and social prestige; but most of all his authority over his subordinates on account of his bookish and bespectacled past, and his undiminished command of language. In short, this job of his. A job which he soon came secretly to flaunt as the banner of his pride. As if in virtue of his intimacy with those rustling, odorous, snow-white children of cellulose which he was distributing for the use of innumerable unknowns on every desk in the country he was not merely a paid supplier but an indispensable accomplice. Fantasies of course, at which he is the first to smile. All the same, he could never have imagined that such an occupation would give him so much pleasure. Pleasure, I mean, like the pleasure of eating, making love, or sleeping. With a sense of contented fatigue at the end of the day, when the workers had gone home and he lingered on with Licausi and Tirrò, talking about the football pools. As they talked they would lean on the parapet of the bridge, matching their words to the soliloquy of the water below, that sounded like the distant song of some prison inmate. For the weeds on either bank had grown so high as practically to gag their prisoner. Tomorrow, they said every evening, they would send someone to clear the weeds away, with a rope around him as a safety measure; and this if only to call the bluff of that trifling rivulet that gave itself the airs of a river.*

*Tomorrow . . . but would it be worth the trouble? A growth so untamed, with such stubborn roots, would be up again in no time, and in a couple of weeks they would be back at square one. Apart from the fact that, save for bothersome gnats and a slight stench of rotting vegetation, the view from the bridge was so picturesque it would be a pity to spoil it. Especially at this hour, at the day's end, of all the hours of the day the tenderest and most seraphic, when up the steep hillside the first vapours of evening are already spreading, while from the sky serenity descends upon the black chimney-pots, the red roofs, the deserted courtyards, penetrating the innermost rooms, and where machines, switched off at last, seem huddled together asleep like weary mules . . .*

*It has got late. Lo Surdo has remained there standing motionless, looking and thinking. Soon the night shift will arrive and set the machinery in motion again. But not soon enough to prevent him standing, feet planted firmly apart, for a last time before his property, to bask in it, to dwell upon it in his mind, to run over the memorable events of the day, the orders received, the profits, the losses, the errors, the welcome surprises . . .*

*The same thing every day at this hour. With no witnesses to his mental balance-sheet other than Licausi, Tirrò and an Alsatian universally and unimaginatively baptized Bow-wow, who after a few seconds of angry vigilance engages in long, fruitless duels with his own shadow, and even longer snoozes in one or another of the dustheaps there in the yard.*

*The same thing every day at this hour. Plus, on this occasion, the sickening echo of that voice:*

"Priparassi cinquanta miliuna" . . .


At this point I re-read and assess my performance. With the astute readers of the "Spyglass" it should go down fairly well: one senses in it a prudent respect for the threatened property, a rejection of any persecution of a shady nature, an implicit demand for law and order. Such as simultaneously to satisfy both the possessors of goods and the preachers of Goodness. Yet into this story of slow, troubled thoughts, of actions as swift as they are brutal, I fear I may have introduced certain lyrical notes, psychological ramblings, roundabout orations which, if I myself find them unsatisfactory, I can only imagine how much less they will please the protagonist, who has encouraged me in this undertaking solely in the hope that, once having been aired in the newspapers, his case will thereby benefit at the assizes.

I therefore proceed with greater caution, hastening matters along, and in order to catch their tone by re-reading the crime reports in the "Spyglass". To what small advantage you may see below.

## Serious Narrative – Part Two

*Some ugly warnings followed: the car with all four tyres slashed, inside the locked garage and with no sign of breaking and entering; the disappearance of Bow-wow, and two days later the discovery of his head in the factory, inside a cast-iron bowl between the knives of the rag-grinding machine. A* mise-en-scène *which Lo Surdo found as repulsive as it was spectacular. There was no doubt that the animal had been decapitated elsewhere, that the decision to place the grisly remains among those deadly blades was an extra, a luxury which, while allusively reinforcing the intimidation, appeared to have been dictated by some perverse artistic streak.*

*There came another message:* "Priparassi sittanta miliuna." *So it was seventy million now, but though he answered "no" with less vehemence he still didn't go to the police. He already knew what they would suggest: pretend to agree, set an ambush, catch them red-handed . . . And he knew what the upshot would be: no one would meet the appointment, the warnings would get ever more insolent and cruel until he finally broke down.*

*He spent day after day in fearful suspense. He walked the streets of the town seeking the shadow of the few stunted trees and the over-hanging balconies; and he felt alone as never before, the helpless target of a hundred hostile eyes hidden behind the shutters. Suddenly, contrary to all previous illusions, he realized that everyone was against him, that his sudden, solitary wealth in a community of paupers had first provoked scandal and then malicious envy. He therefore broke with the habits of a lifetime and steeled himself to discuss it with his wife. "Pay up," advised Giuliana, "before the price goes up again or they kill you. Pay up." He paid.*

*A few quiet months went by. But he had trouble in mind, a permanent clot of regret, a fury of mortification. He worked his fingers to the bone to keep the firm afloat and make up for the lost money, gnawed at by rancour because every extra effort was a tax* imposed on him by them, *the three black-coated tax-collectors with their disguised voices, of whom he had glimpsed, through the holes in their balaclavas, only their ferocious eyes, sharp as pinpoints. The rendezvous had occurred at night, at the place where three roads meet by the Burnt-out House, and he had gone home on foot, leaving his car there as they commanded him to, and carrying the floppy hold-all that he had brought there bulging with banknotes.*

*There was peace, therefore, for several months. Until the telephone started to torture him with further demands. And this time there was a novelty: the voice was a different voice, the claims were even higher, and there were many indications that this was another and a rival gang.*

*"Go ahead and kill each other off first," growled Lo Surdo into the mouthpiece. "I'll be the prize for the winner."*

*"You'll go first," replied the voice. "*Facimu prima a ammazzari a tia.*" A calm, implacable voice, without inflections, but slightly grey and metallic. The way robots talk in movies.*

*The man did not want to pay, nor could he do so. And the paper-mill burnt down one night and you might think it was the feast of the patron saint, with lovely great tongues of flame and a roar of roasting paper worthy of a Hollywood sound-track. The whole town came running, in pyjamas and dressing-gowns, to enjoy the sight from the terrace of Cozzo d'Apollo, while two volunteer firemen did a circus act with hosepipes, more intent on squirting each other than disturbing the blaze.*

*The main walls of the buildings remained, the rest went up in smoke. The machinery, reduced to blackened scrap-iron, looked like bits of sculpture waiting to be packed off to the Biennial Exhibition of Ironwork in Gubbio, useless now for any other purpose.*

*It was then that Lo Surdo moved to Rome and took up lodgings with us, to be on the spot to wage a war without quarter on the United Insurance, but harried from the start by the charge of having himself* caused the disaster in order to collect on the policy. He was forced to sell the still-smoking ruins to Tirrò, Licausi and an anonymous third party. And it seems that these three, having put the dump back on its feet, were earning good money.

He, on the contrary, is paying his way as best he can, plagued by lawyers' fees, and egged on by his intrepid wife, even more ravening than he is. She has her suspicions, too: "How the factory is booming nowadays," she whispered to me before stepping into the corridor and pulling the door to behind her. "It seems the new owners don't have the problems we had. And it's a mystery how they got the money to buy and restore the factory. When they paid us in front of the notary I seemed to see our own bundles of brand-new hundred-thousand-lire notes, fastened with the same green elastic bands . . . "

"You mean to tell me . . . ?" I gasped, grasping her arm.

"I mean to tell you," she replied, and slid back into the room.

And here the story would be breasting the tape, if I did not feel the need to make premature disclosure of its ironical-tragical appendix. This occurred a week later, when Enrico Lo Surdo was surprised and arrested in a public telephone booth while (a handkerchief held to his mouth and a clothes-peg on his nose) he hissed to Licausi and Tirrò the very same fatal words with which his own catastrophe had begun: "Priparassi cinquanta miliuna" . . .

# SIX

# Strange Doings in the Building

*Wednesday, August 23rd*

Thinking over the Lo Surdo affair, what a cautionary tale it contains! It teaches us that, whereas a *naïf* painter can aspire to emulate a professional painter, anyone who turns to crime without an adequate apprenticeship is likely to find himself up a gum tree. However much he puts his heart into it, a gentleman will always remain a clumsy beginner at evil-doing. It has to be his bread and butter, as my father would say, before his skin can cast off the sorry birthmark and vice of honesty.

Conclusion: on account of its intrinsic moral lesson the story I have just told does not seem to me complete rubbish, and I've half a mind to submit it to the "Spyglass". A little embarrassing, perhaps, because of the obvious contradiction I'm falling into. For to put it bluntly, it is all very well to want to withdraw from the vanities and vexations of the world, but the fact is that every morning the absurd but chronic anguish of empty pockets reminds me yet again that I still need money, if only for a sleeping pill or a laxative. Not to mention the thousand other bonds that fetter me to everydayness, and clip the wings of my pride and liberty. This is why I secretly envy those who have succeeded in making a legend and an historic paradigm of their own self-segregation. I think of Iacopo da Pontormo in a ramshackle garret, as he lowers and hauls up the basket with his provisions, then immediately closets himself again with his solitary fantasies . . . I think of Bobby Fischer, unvanquished champion, in a bar in Minnesota or wherever, losing an endless series of East-Indians against himself on a pocket chessboard . . . I think of Glenn Gould, at one with his keyboard in a sealed room from which the least draught was excluded, along with all intruders barring the shade of J. S. Bach, who dwells in his mind.

Three superlative agoraphobes . . . Three sick men? Perish the thought! Simply seekers after solitude as a bandage or medicinal remedy to existence, but none the less even they constrained to sacrifice some of their sequestered hours to the demands of society or the community, and who knows how often to betray the completeness of their own innermost being. Far less often than I do, needless to say, and to make a comparison between us one would require a gauge such as is used to measure the motions of the earth and sea: a force-five solitary am I, whereas they are force-nine! Nor must we forget the greatest of them all, he who paradoxically sought his Trappist cell amongst the peoples of distant lands, where he found adventures, and dangers, and death . . . the fugitive with winged feet – him it is I speak of, and his insolent challenge to the aged bastions of Europe. Maybe only to cadge a few nights as a slave-trader beneath moons more lunar than any in Charleville or Paris, there amid the rocks of the Jebel! . . .

Very well, many thanks for not interrupting me. Every so often I suffer from these excesses of self-indulgent grandiloquence. Especially after rolling in the dirt of the day and then using it to stuff the memoirs you see before you. As you will have noticed, I am pushing them ahead with some trouble, never free of the fear that I might have to bring them to a sudden end, with three dots or a dash . . . It is widely known that Incompleteness is the Muse closest to my heart (my entire life has been a coitus interruptus, a series of sprints halfway between one hurdle and the next, a sequence of ineluctable sterilities), but this Muse would not suffice without the unravelling of time around me, the way it crumbles into fleeting moments and incidents, as when motes of dust dance in a golden beam that strikes them for an instant and is then eclipsed by a cloud.

Thus do I see the days pass by and perish. Today it is still fine weather. Tomorrow will come the north winds and the mists, once more I shall hear the receding hiss of tyres on wet asphalt, colder stars will shine in the sky. We of Flower City live rooted in inertia, like a shipload of cholera cases quarantined in a harbour. We are self-sufficient if it comes to that, since supplies are not lacking. Every morning the newsagent dumps his stack of dailies on the doorstep, the milkman leaves his cartons on every threshold. All that is needed for the provisions of every family is a telephone call to the nearest supermarket and a few minutes later an assistant arrives with a laden trolley . . .

As for the postman, he doesn't even bother to distribute the mail, but knocks only at my door, hands me the stack of letters and leaves it up to me to get on with it. I willingly assent: it is a pleasant distraction to make a note of the addresses of the senders, weigh the envelopes in my hand, sniff the perfume, infer or dream up farces and tragedies on the basis of two or three ambiguous words on a postcard from the Engadine . . . Like this morning.

The card, addressed to Signor Torquato Marino, alias Mariposa, reads: "My butterfly, Mariposa querida! I am brimming with honey and await you! Greetings from Skyros." The signature beneath is Achilles, but even further down is a scribble that might well be read as Patroclus. On the front of the card is a view of the baths at Tarasp, against a background of rather gloomy woods. Skyros my foot!

It is with some hesitancy that I go up to the fifth floor. At this time of day Mariposa is sleeping and I don't want to wake her (I am opting for the "her" once and for all, though not without embarrassment). A chink of light under the door gives me the courage to call her softly by name. The answer is a warbled "Come in!"

I step into the room, a bombonnière of frills, slippers, wigs, screens, rustling silks. Hanging in the air is a sweetish odour, a mixture of talcum powder and Paco Rabanne.

Mariposa is undressing and, despite my complete forbearance, I feel a slight shudder of repugnance, not so much at the sight but the sounds, the snap of elastic on the stocking-tops, the crackle of nylon scraped by fingernails, the twitterings and simperings of her voice:

"Ciao, my handsome Newsrag, what's up?"

It's her peculiar habit to call me "Newsrag", in memory of my journalistic past, just as she calls the fortune-teller "Tarot", the Greek "Carpet", Biscegli "Trumpet", Lo Surdo "Paper-mill" and so forth, each according to some attribute or qualifying fact in their lives.

"This is for you," I say.

She takes the card between two fingers, reads it, reads it again, bursts into tears. I watch huge tears run down her fat cheeks, ruin her make-up, run off her chin and bog down among the wrinkles of her neck. The situation is such as to make a man wish he were elsewhere.

She catches on in a flash: "Don't go away, Newsrag," she begs, drying her eyes on the hem of her petticoat. "Just look what a rotter he is." And she shows me the card, asks me to read it, as if I didn't know it by heart already. "Look there," (pointing to the second, indecipherable signature), "he's with someone else and he wants me to know it!"

This would have been followed by an emotional outburst that in the past I often found touching, but which now leaves me cold. I forestall her: "Tomorrow, I haven't got time today," and I flee into the corridor where the inevitable Garaffa is at work and does not deign to look at me. Hoisted on a step-ladder which the boy Maurizio is pretending to steady for him, he is using a magnifying glass to examine the ceiling, at a point where a swelling in the whitewash, a sort of incrustation, is visible to the naked eye. He is unaware that his faithless assistant is sniggering behind his back – that same Maurizio whom a few hours before I had caught tearing the warning strips of tape from the cracks in the wall.

I leave them to their vaudeville double-act and devote myself to the thought of Mariposa. Feeling, in moderation, remorse for having left her in the abundance of her tears, as harmless as summer rains. Yes, I say remorse, because in her way, and with frequent remissions of mood that even extend to uncontrollable laughter, she suffers. The postcard was certainly sent her by Redaelli, the former music-hall star with whom she lived for six years, and to whose influence she owes, if nothing else, the defiant resolution not to hide herself away any more. With him she engaged in Homeric battles, on account of their reciprocal betrayals and divergent culinary tastes. Then came the break-up and from her ex-lover, every summer, when he goes touring the world with a new companion, a stream of telephonic, telegraphic and above all epistolatory sneers, which she collects in an album like relics.

I have met this epistolomaniac, having interviewed him after a show at a time when I was the "Spyglass" theatre critic. And how he did go on about having been the inventor, long before

*Cabaret*, of that number with a dancer dressed on one side as a man and on the other as a woman, who as he dances seems to duel with himself, dazzled by the spotlights in the act of challenging, loving and hating himself in one single ambiguous body, while the black-and-white face, and the gestures now of frenzy now of languor, betoken premonitions of death. A *persona* fifty per cent tragic and a hundred per cent hysterical was Redaelli on the stage. Off it he was a wide-stepping sinner whose laughter hushed the rapids of the Rhine and was renowned in all the plushy reception rooms of all the *hôtels particuliers* from Venice to Hamburg.

So I was thinking of Mariposa, of Redaelli, and of how tortuous is the nature of man. Or rather of Nature with a capital N. On account of how she weaves so closely together the rule and the exception. I wonder if Placido isn't right, with his theory that one's innards are attached to all existing phenomena, if it is true that even the wonky tempo of my heart, with its alternating flurries and slow marches, is enslaved less by a whim than by a law, curse it . . . Does the same hold good for the ambiguity of Mariposa? Is it a disorder within an order? Or an order within a disorder? "I don't dress up, I simply dress," she told me once, meaning that she dressed as a woman not to make herself other than she was, but for the pleasure of becoming herself, of show- ing herself as she really was, by some fallacious imposture.

"Your mother . . . " I began, my head still fresh from studying Viennese doctors.

"My mother? She has nothing to do with it. Even though the memory of her breast, the soft warmth of the flesh in which I buried my face, the sweetish taste of the milk on my lips, are all still alive in me, in a season of joy and terror. As it is in you, as it is in all of us . . . "

And she also said that before becoming aware of her tendency she had loved a woman, and in fact several. "Never requited," she added. "I knew in my heart that I was just false coinage, and felt the honey-sweet heresy of being one of them. I loved them, but they didn't love me. I had to turn myself into a woman to be able to love myself again, to be two persons in one, the lover and the loved one . . . "

Now – and I cannot suppress a smile – Redaelli sends her into a fit of jealousy with a postcard from a supposed Skyros where he is teamed up with a so-called Patroclus. While she is walking the streets in the hope of putting a few pennies by. Her great dream is in the realm of surgery: it seems that in Berlin they can work miracles.

On my way to my next base my thoughts turn to my marriage and my wife Rosa. Since we parted, not a word from her. I suppose she doesn't even know where I am, what I'm doing. And I know almost as little about her. One of the most ill-assorted and random couples you could imagine. She was the owner of a sports shop: skis, rowing-machines, rackets, harpoon guns and rubber suits for every kind of embolizable and drownable skin-diver; I was a freelance journalist and aspiring author, bewitched by the most abstruse and metaphysical dilemmas, and from very early days aware of having deceived myself as to her patience as a listener, imagining enraptured attention where there was only a mask and behind it a void. All the same, we would have stayed together until God knows when if she'd been less tiresome, less off-putting . . . If she hadn't had the habit of interrupting herself in the middle of every sentence with an inquisitorial "Eh?" that called me in question right out of the blue, and caught me napping in my philosophical slumbers. If she had left fewer hairs in the washbasin and fewer curlicues in the bidet . . . But there she was, every morning, in a Madame Butterfly kimono, prattling away without drawing breath about the previous evening's canasta, her married cousin in Monfalcone, the latest episode of *Beautiful* . . .

And there was I muttering under my breath: "Don't take it so hard, Tommaso, don't let it crack your nerve, sear your soul. You can do her in whenever you please, the flat is full of rat poison, lengths of cord . . . "

"Eh?" she would ask.

"What, me? I haven't uttered a word."

Just to think that she seemed to me a conquest, when I met her in the shop, standing behind the counter. She seemed an apple right out of Paradise, a woman ready to sop up my blather like blotting paper. That's how I trapped her: a few honeyed words then my hands on her at once, her clothes scattered to the four winds in the storeroom of the shop and a great tumbling and deflating of lilos and rubber rings . . .

*Rosa*, *rosae* from then on, for the rest of my life. Rosa with her nasal voice, a breastbone like a flatiron and a coriander seed for a brain. And it could be the case that everything about her was beginning to turn my stomach, but every time I "did" her I had the sensation of ploughing my way through a cave in the Carso, caught in a karstic cul-de-sac of pumice-stone. Although she, odourless and flavourless as she was, and incapable of squeezing out a single droplet of encouraging pleasure, had the nerve to contort herself and scratch me during the act of sex, and to whimper and mew and huff and puff ("it's good, it's good") that you'd have thought she was Messalina's cat. Whereas it was all too obvious that she went to all that trouble out of mere coquetry and submissiveness, and that she'd studied the part in the sex insert distributed in sealed envelopes along with copies of "Eva Bazar". Having dispatched my duty I was left with a sticky mess of boiled sweets and lipstick in my mouth. And impressed on my pupil the close-up of a pallid earlobe, of a half-moon-shaped earring partly hidden between two locks of hair, somewhat to the north of a violet satin shoulder strap. Oof! I went on grumbling to myself until far into the night: wan-blond hair and forebodings of colostrum, if that's really the word for it . . . Yes, because to cap it all at this point she happened to get pregnant, and the flat was always cram-full of girlfriends she had picked up God knows where, on the underground, at the hairdresser's, and all of them from her part of the world, Rovigo, Sottomarina . . . Boisterous lasses with painted faces and an affected way of walking, all wriggle and *pas de deux*. When I heard them arriving in a gaggle on a Sunday it sent me up the wall. They, on the contrary, adored me, so they told Rosa: "Sweetie-pie, what a lucky one you are to have a chum for a husband. Heaven knows how proud you must feel to be seen strolling arm-in-arm together." This at least, spoken in an unlikely mixture of Trastevere and the Veneto dialect, is how I pictured their get-togethers, all intent on cosseting her, knitting away at baby jumpers, the tray of sweetmeats within reach. Or else I saw them as petrified, stupefied Parcae peering at the monoscope of the colour TV. The entire Po delta went into mourning when she miscarried.

Peace be unto her and unto me: it's all been over for three years now, and I have not a single regret. To my new life, a poor thing but mine own, I have become so accustomed as to have no wish ever to change it. I go so far as to think that a different and grander destiny would dazzle me, like a miner or an astronaut, when they emerge from their pit or spaceship into the light of day . . .

Busy with these thoughts I worm my way into the lift. Every so often it actually works, and I find it now crowded with strangers, a little band of Jehovah's Witnesses: beards of the

Prophets, bags of pamphlets under their arms, a strong urge to catechize. Among them a fanatical blond girl whose pony-tail, squashed in as we are, whips me across the face like a handful of ears of corn. They get out disappointed, they have knocked at so many doors, but few were opened and everyone was irritated. Out of sheer mischief I direct them to the philosopher, I foresee a tasty wrangle and regret I can't be present. I bid them farewell, for having distributed the mail my only wish is to get back to my street-watching sentry-box, my life-raft for the forthcoming Flood, the sole umbilical cord between me and history. I say history on the assumption that what is happening out there in the sunshine is history and what is happening in here is mere journalism, and not the other way round . . . Apart from that I have with me, on loan from our trumpeter, a new cassette to listen to. Ten numbers by Bix Beiderbecke, dating back to the days of "Singing the Blues" and "Way Down Yonder in New Orleans".

I find the door of my residence open and the room jam-packed. Up and down this tower block there's a positive migration of peoples today. I now realize why God's propagandists came away empty-handed: most of the inhabitants were here with me, a downright delegation. There was no resistance, my home is like a free port because I always leave the key in the lock.

"Good morning," "Good morning," just a few brief greetings, and it's obvious they're extremely het-up. They are all people with whom I am on fairly friendly terms, even if with one of them, the glacial Leah, I would like to be on friendlier ones. Since I possess only three chairs, and ramshackle to boot, I propose a "standing session". My play on words passes unnoticed, they are all talking at once in choral indignation and I am taken unawares by one of my recurrent "mental reserves": right from the very first words (a protest against an arbitrary order of Mundula's affixed to the notice-board in the entrance-hall, demanding a large special contribution to some very urgent restoration work, under pain of eviction) I freeze up in my catastrophic "Well, so what?" while my cheeks begin to burn. I babble, and with horrid misgiving become aware of the shortcomings of my resolution to maintain a haughty detachment in the face of the inevitable pressures of life beyond my powers of prohibition or consent. Not to mention the fact that I have nothing to do with the present case. I am Mundula's uninformed lackey, and that's how I earn my subsistence. What do these people want from me? Am I to be the spokesman for a mutiny that scarcely concerns me? Well, really!

I attempt an answer, venturing on a hazardous analogy: "Do you know the myth of Atlas?" I begin. "We learn at school that he carries the earth on his shoulders, but no one explains where he plants his feet. He is outside the terrestrial globe yet lives in it. Now I am practically outside this condominium, yet you want me to carry it on my back, attics and all . . . "

Here I get stuck, lose my grip on the analogy. The best I can do is shut up.

And impulsively to my aid comes Leah. She has a voice like a Hyblaean flute in the afternoon of a faun, a prelude in B flat with a humming of bees and running water and reeds as a soothing accompaniment. "Never mind Atlas. You haven't got the muscles for it," says she, in such a familiar way that I almost faint. "Perhaps a less far-fetched comparison will suit you better. You know those painters who put themselves into the picture they are painting, and are both in it and out of it at the same time? Well, the same thing is true of you. You are one us and at the same time you aren't. You live like a phoney hermit in this extra-territorial hovel of yours, you don't pay a penny and yet it's you who harass us in your role of rent-collector and paymaster. Make up your mind:

are you inside the picture or out of it? With or against us."

Suddenly dumbstruck with love, I gaze at her adoringly.

She continues, and now her voice puts forth more prickles than a prickly-pear: "As for that Mundula, I am not ashamed to admit it, the day before yesterday he called me into his office, said that for me and my father some agreement might be reached, and he slipped his hand inside my blouse . . . "

On the instant all eyes are riveted on her bosom, on the blouse that covers it. White it was and duly swelling, more than duly unbuttoned, offered like the Host to a troop of communicants.

"I'll kill him if he tries it again," added the girl hastily. "With my own hands."

Once again she captured my gaze. Her hands were very pale, like the rest of her, with the fingers of a pianist and nails without varnish but like little pink gems. As sharp as toy scalpels in the hands of a small girl torturing birds, or some such sadistic child. At this point we saw the printer give a start and make for his daughter. He appeared uncertain whether to embrace her or what. Finally he made up his mind and gave her a resounding and spectacular slap, straight out of the movies. "That," he burst out, "is for speaking when it was my place to do so. And for saying things you haven't told me. You oughtn't even to have come here. In here you're like a flower on a dungheap. I don't want you to sully your mouth again with them, with anyone. I'll deal with Mundula. He'll pay for this, by God he will."

Leah did not lose her composure, in fact quite unexpectedly she smiled. Then "Goodbye, goodbye to everyone," she said, and her exit could have been that of Greta Garbo. "Let's wait till the day after tomorrow, at the tenants' meeting," said Crisafulli calmly. Then, to me: "If you don't feel like asserting our rights for us we'll do it ourselves on that occasion. But not," (and he was so peremptory and solemn that I couldn't tell whether or not he was joking) "before I have recited you my latest monologue, *The Filibuster*. A masterpiece. After that, very well, let's murder Mundula."

"But couldn't we write to Mr Cacciola?" protested Adriana. "After all, he's the owner and he might be more generous. My cards speak as well of him as they speak ill of Mundula. For Mundula all the Major Arcana came out, the Fool first of all, then the Hermit. Now, if the Hermit is Mulè, the Fool is Mundula, there's no way round it. All the more so because immediately afterwards came the sixteenth card, which is the Tower. And lastly, upside down, the thirteenth card, and you all know what that is."

"And what on earth is it?" I asked, not having the first notion of such matters. Adriana did not answer at once, then: "It's . . . ," she began, but broke off as a light shower from the damp ceiling sprinkled her hair, a powdering of decaying flaking that turned us all white without hurting anyone. But it served to rekindle the chorus of complaints: "There you are! That's the sort of dump we're living in. And he has the nerve to come cadging more money!"

# SEVEN

# The Get-together

*Thursday, August 24th*

The meeting has broken up and here I am lying on my little bed, listening. At regular intervals there comes a rumbling in the roadway, and my few drinking glasses clink together. It's the tram on the outer circle line making its presence felt. I imagine it crammed with a sticky and frantic mob. How much better off am I here in the cool, a wanted man whom no one is looking for; a fugitive absent from any "Have you seen this face?" notices; in peace with myself at last, and with mankind, even with God . . . content to turn my back on him respectfully, after shaking my fist at him all my life long.

At least until yesterday. Today I am having some troubled moments, and foresee others more troubled still. All the fault of this perdition of the heart that I have called love, partly to brag, partly because I don't know what else to call it. Indeed I feel I've been ambushed by a transport as intense as it is hybrid and questionable. Imagine a prospector who thinks he sees a diamond in a rock but, just to make sure, has to cleanse it of all the gangue and mud. In the same way I find myself struggling against the mass of philosophical dross that in me is wont to stifle the simplest impulse, and all the more energetically insofar as it clashes with a gigantic emotion such as is coming to birth, or is already born in me.

Leah, therefore. Younger than me by thirty years, seen at close quarters only twice, and always under the wing of the terrible paternal collar (watch it, that's a literary allusion!) . . . All the same, a priceless opportunity to study *d'après nature* on my own vile body the stratagems, the guilelessness, the advancements, the disasters, the thrills, the ecstasies of the aforesaid blighted sentiment, in its classic variant of an ageing man falling head over heels for a young chick.

We shall start with a preliminary inspection of the subject. Let us see: the girl is beautiful, but more an apparition with sealed lips than a sensual presence. Nor, as long as she kept her mouth shut, did I pay her more attention than that of a desire as vague as it was variable. Ergo, it was her voice, and the cavatinas carolled by that voice, that lit the fuse of this explosion in me.

A contralto voice that changes its inflections every instant, eliciting from them a wicked titillation of the nerves, like fingers running through one's hair or brushing the back of one's neck . . . After which I immediately felt the urge to play the old male game of mentally undressing her; a game I much enjoyed in early adolescence, but which (due to distaste and growing up) I later lost interest in. So that, poor sod that I am, aided only by pure fantasy, I strip her of her clothes and judiciously scrutinize her, from a neck of the most slender gracefulness, such as to tempt the most fastidious of stranglers, to the breasts – two brimming goblets made to measure for a pair of sensitive hands; from the musical flair of her hips to the gentle declivity of her belly, as warm as a new-born baby's cheek; from the black copse to the roseate petals of her pubes, and thence to the noble splendour of her legs . . . In short, one plus one plus one, the quality of the factors in this sum total is such as to hold up the viewing process at every moment. The same thing as happens when I press the remote control that freezes a videocassette at a favourite frame, and I stare at it with the pride and remorse of having suspended life and time. Just so was Leah and her toy theatre in my mind: an impassive statue that I felt I must oust from its pedestal if it cost me my life, either by possessing her or by killing her or by seizing a scalpel and excising her from my mind. All of them extreme options and not at all up my street. All the more so because I know from long experience that, when I do burn, my lust is as ephemeral as a votive candle. However, before my flame dies I am obliged to seek some kind of outlet, even if my behaviour is that of a beardless youth with frenzied senses. Thus, the next morning, at the hour when the printer takes the tram to work in the centre, you may see me outside the girl's door, my finger hovering near the bellpush. I am not there to declare my passion, good Lord no. I wish merely to hear her, nose her, brush her arm with my fingertips again, and in a word do everything I can to pull her out of her cloud up there and so perhaps forget her. Because love is nearly always love for a cloud, and rain or sunshine is enough to disperse it (in my breviary of myths I have always relished that of Ixion, who fell in love with a goddess and was deceived into making love to her cloud-image. Well, what do we all do, when we love a woman, if not mistake a Nephele for a Hera, ending up broken on a wheel revolving for all eternity, each in his own domestic hell?).

I press the bell, therefore. Once, twice. And the third time it opens a cautious crack, secured by the chain. Without a trace of make-up, Leah's face is of a pallor to be found only in a film library, a 1920s Theda Bara after being bitten by Dracula.

She is wearing a white dressing-gown, gives me a look of astonished hauteur, but addresses me in familiar fashion: "What d'you want?"

At this point I spin out of control. Meaning that although for years I have subjected myself to the strictest self-analysis, and believe I know every closet and crafty false-bottomed drawer of my character, I now suddenly realize that within me I harbour an impulsive, unpredictable alien. For in fact a question – the most indiscreet, the least premeditated – erupts from my breast, born of the occult manoeuvres of an unknown hand, all unbeknownst to my conscious mind, which hears it with astonishment and horror: "Who is Buozzi for you? Is he really your father? Is he your lover? Or both at the same time?"

I have unwittingly hit the nail on the head. Instead of yelling or weeping she undoes the chain, lets me in, closes the door and, standing face to face with me, as if this is all she's been waiting for, she lets herself go:

"My father? Who knows? He was my mother's lover and shared her bed with her rightful husband. When I was born they weren't sure which was the father. Then, during a motor-trip a fatal accident did for the married couple, leaving me, a little girl, and the lover as the only survivors. And with him I remained, growing up as his daughter or stepdaughter or adopted daughter, you name it. I've asked him a thousand times for us to go together to a doctor specializing in these chemical things, to find out – they say one can – if I am of his blood or not. He hasn't ever wanted to go, he prefers the uncertainty that enables him to keep me isolated and not only that . . . "

"In short, you sleep together?" I am forced to ask brutally.

"What do *you* think?" she asks in turn, piqued. "In any case it's none of your business. I can only say that if I knew where to go I'd get out."

That makes two of them. After the story of Tir playing a physically impossible Peeping Tom on his own sister, all we needed was this piece of filth, a presumed father with his daughter. It shakes my fragile peace of mind. What a sad muddle is the heart of every man, and how hard it is for me to avoid a pang of universal, helpless pity! My first impulsive daring collapses, and I can do no better than blurt out "I'll help you" and, stumbling over the "Welcome" on the doormat, I make it out through the door.

I don't meet a soul in any of the many corridors. The odd thing about this year is that so far no one has come back from their holidays. In previous years, from mid-August on, it was all a riot of festive homecomings: peeled noses, salt-parched cheeks, pullovers knotted round waists, multicoloured flimsies swathing coffee-coloured legs . . . The building was repopulated in the batting of an eyelid, the first school satchels appeared in the hands of the most zealous of the gang of infants. This year there's nothing of the kind. In fact there are alarming signs: letters from tenants terminating their agreements, a few departures already announced, a general silence. As if they had decided *en masse* to move house noiselessly, deserting us overnight. Thinking it over, it begins to worry me. I go to Mundula to seek enlightenment. He tells me the whole thing must spring from a false alarm about the soundness of the building, started by that half-wit Garaffa. "We are living in a solid rock," he proclaims, rapping his knuckles against a pillar. "And in any case," he adds, "if that crackpot of an engineer had any serious doubts he'd have been the first to run for it, instead of fooling around with compasses and goniometers, and maybe even sending in a bill for his professional services . . . "

"Yes, but what does the management intend to do about it?"

"We'll thrash the matter out at the meeting. To anyone who doesn't come back I'll give a week's grace, if he's in arrears. After that the furniture goes out of the window. To make sure this is feasible I've already been in touch with the civil-engineering office. It'll all go like a dream."

It's clear that Mundula is furious, to judge from this tirade. Moreover his brow is scarlet and the veins in his neck are swelling; his nose, craggy and Cyranesque from birth, is wrinkling like ropy lava ("My mother," he once confessed to me, "went to watch a boxing match when she was a few months pregnant. A Basque pugilist, by the name of Paolo Uzcudum, whose nose was bashed cockeyed, made a great impression on her"). A character I have not yet made out, is Mundula. If there is any truth (and why should she have lied?) in what Leah said about him and his lascivious approaches, although scarcely credible in such a waddling fatty, one must deduce a streak of double-dealing and repressed violence that I have not discerned.

However that may be, the drift of the conversation leaves me worried: if news of the stampede should come to the ears of the others, and the building should be deserted, what would become of me?

My thoughts go back to a snowy evening last winter, and the picture that suddenly materialized in the rectangle of my little window: the face of a tramp who had fallen to the ground just the other side of the grating, maybe drunk, maybe dying of a heart attack. His small, enquiring eyes, unbearably blue, were staring straight at me. I remember the long beard, stiff with icicles, the quivering of his chin, the cheeks rapidly turning the colour of slate. And the damp fag-end still hanging from a corner of his mouth.

I stayed rooted to the spot for several minutes, as if watching a silent film. I overcame the impulse to dash outside and help (of my moral unworthiness I will provide further examples later on); then a crowd gathered round him, I heard the siren of an ambulance . . .

Will I end up that way too? Does danger really threaten my holiday of peaceful mediocrity? Once before, in my youth, before getting a job on the paper, I lived by my wits, doing anything that came my way: an extra at Cinecittà, clad in leafy boughs before the castle of Dunsinane; attendant to an ex-Bersaglieri general in a wheelchair; auctioneer of fake Dali paintings on local TV; sandwich man touting anything from cakes of soap to variety shows . . . But I was young then, full of whims and fancies. Nowadays if I lose this daily bread . . . Well, we'll see. "In the meanwhile," I say to Mundula in a spirit of co-operation, "why go on tolerating those drug sessions up there?"

I'm referring to a group of young men "of good family" who rent an attic for the sole purpose of shooting themselves with drugs, not sleeping there and paying when they can, so much each, and more often than not they can't. If you meet them they all seem to be the same person, bearded, long-haired, bespectacled, with the slither of a yellow snake deep in their sleepy pupils . . .

"Easy does it," says Mundula. "You don't know the latest. They gave notice yesterday." And with a pontifical gesture he dismisses me.

After this conversation I return to my room disconcerted and in need of air. So much so that I have an urge to break with my habits and take a walk outside. My last outing was with Tir on that useless pilgrimage in search of his lost Matilde. It's of him that I think now, for company and reciprocal distraction from our worries. I find him unexpectedly cheerful and talkative: Cesare is once again at his side, and with a more grown-up air, contrition mingled with roguishness. I don't know how he justified his disappearance, but certainly the blind man does not seem to have connected it with his sister's simultaneous vanishing trick. Especially as he is able triumphantly to exhibit a greetings telegram. From Taormina, God help her.

So out we go, and the arrangement is to see an old movie of Bresson's (*Lancelot*) at a fourth-showing cinema only a couple of hundred metres from home. On the way I would really like to tell him about me and Leah, but he forestalls me. He lowers his voice and starts to take me into his confidence. He always has a lot of fine birds in his game-bag. This time the revelation concerns a sex party the scenes of which he has been hired to photograph without witnessing them. A get-together, as far as in his blindness he is able to understand, involving bigshots in the worlds of business, politics, entertainment, a whole breath-taking Almanac de Gotha, an élite of indolent ministers, fake Luxembourgeois financiers, papal princes. Along with them were the best paid lays in the city, as well as two outsiders, a pair of nymphets scarcely out of school. They had just run away from home and had been picked up at Castropretorio – a soldiers' camp and hang-out since Ancient Roman days.

In my own way I'm a bit of a moralist and, still smarting from the case of Buozzi & Daughter, I can't restrain my indignation:

"But you . . . Where do you come in?"

"They pay well," he replied calmly, "and if I don't do it they'll find someone else. I'm running no risks: what the eye doesn't see the heart doesn't grieve over. Whatever happens the only witness is my camera, and at the end I hand over all my rolls. All except one," and here he lowers his voice almost to a whisper, "that I slip into a pocket for my archives."

"A fine viper they're nursing in their bosom," I observe.

"On the contrary, I'm as silent as the grave. And blind as I am I suit them down to the ground, I haven't seen anything so I can't accuse anyone. I have nothing to fear either, whatever happens I'm in the clear. Ignorance isn't a sin. As far as I know I could have been photographing the marriage at Cana . . . "

His reasoning hangs together but fails to convince me. Not

least because the story doesn't end there. When he had finished taking pictures and handed over the material, Tir was politely given a lift home, and it was all love and kisses. Except that this morning on the radio he heard a piece of news that made his blood run cold. A girl had been found dead in a doorway, a syringe beside her. She was called Ersilia Trapani and she hailed from the Ciociarìa.

"So what?" I ask, using my habitual interpolation appropriately for once.

"You see, amongst the laughter and the love-play and the obscenities I heard going on around me without seeing anything, I was struck by a joke at the expense of someone they were taking the micky out of because of her Ciociaro accent, and they called by her initials like the child in that film: E.T."

"You mean it was Ersilia Trapani?"

"Well, it's a possibility. Even if the doorway she was found in is over two kilometres . . . "

"From where? From what?"

He was silent for a while, then added: "Listen here, I don't know a thing about the people who hire me, but I do have an idea of where this gathering took place. It's facing a fountain I know the sound of, at the corner of a piazza which my shoes know every cobblestone of. There's a bump I used to stumble over every morning when I lived around those parts."

"What are you thinking of doing?"

"Nothing for this evening. This evening I only want to go to the movie and then think about it a bit."

The audience is very small: a lone figure in the front row with luminous pen and notepad, probably a student of the cinema taking notes in the dark. In any case an oculist's delight, of truly impressive myopia, who at the least whisper of ours hisses an indignant "Shhh!"; whereas on the contrary the three couples of mixed sex who share the auditorium with us show no sign of life, intent as they are on forming pairs of Siamese twins in their seats.

We plunge into the film, and I am immediately struck by the way they have of cutting down the size of the frames, so that all one sees is legs, feet, hooves, the dais of a throne, as if the screen were occupied by a beheaded army. To such an extent that I could be at my habitual games, standing at my peephole watching the people pass. It's all right for Tir, who of course doesn't notice it, but avidly drinks in the sounds and dialogue, in an effort to translate them into figures and actions on the black screen that forbids him to see them. I feel him beside me straining with really touching enthusiasm, and who knows what he is inventing, what story is told him by those galloping hoofbeats in the distance, that clashing of sword blades in the forest, those lovewords of yore . . . More absorbed than I am, he doesn't notice a momentary draught that informs me that the curtain over the entrance behind us has been opened a crack, that someone must have come in or gone out. I glance round to check, and am briefly intrigued by the fact that no new arrivals are to be seen, the seven of before are still only seven: the three couples intent on leeching on to each other, and the seventh holding his glow-worm of a pen and writing, writing, writing.

Perhaps, I think, it is the cashier who has popped her head inside for a moment to get a breath of air-conditioned air, and I settle for this explanation. I look back at the blind man: he is still thrusting out his jaw as if sniffing the wind and clasping the armrests tightly. Then, all of a sudden: "D'you mind if we leave now? I've just thought of something."

I don't ask him what; I simply get up, take him by the arm and guide him up the aisle to the exit. And here we are on the pavement outside the cinema, waiting for the lights to change.

The moment they go green I give him the word and he gets off to a dashing start with his stick under his arm like a lance. I follow him half a step behind – just enough to save me in the split second I see a Kawasaki, crashing the red light against the traffic, bearing down on us. Mingled with the snarl of its engine I hear a creak as of sagging hinges, I see Tir's head practically in smithereens while his body, spread-eagled like a scarecrow's, swirls for a moment in space before smashing against the wall, to print a crimson silhouette on the poster for *Lancelot*.

# EIGHT

# My Prison Life

*Thursday, August 24th. Friday, August 25th*

How demeaning, to make off through the crowd as I did. But any assemblage of people gives me an instant feeling of indignant desolation, and I can't endure it. Nor was the horror of the scene possible to bear for someone with nerves as flimsy as mine. Therefore, even at the risk of arousing suspicion, there was nothing for it at that moment but to take to my heels.

It was not a good idea, and when they picked me up later, red-eyed and distrait in the vicinity of Porta Pia (I'd been walking for ages), it cost me an unmannerly arrest and twelve hours in the cooler waiting to be interrogated on a charge of having avoided giving evidence although informed of the facts. My lack of documents did the rest. The next day I had to have recourse to my ex-boss Bendidio, you can imagine just how willingly, asking him to vouch for me and prevent me getting shot on the spot. But joking apart I didn't come off too badly. I really needed a pause for reflection, removed from any promptings or prejudice. In any case, no stranger to the four walls of a cell and a plank bed, I had no trouble getting used to it, except for regretting the derangement of my evening rituals and the resulting sleepless night, as in the good old days. I had wandered around aimlessly for hours, until my feet were on fire. When at last I sat down at a table in a bar I was seized by one of my moods of glum indifference. What the hell? They had killed a friend, but I sought in vain in myself for some drop of torment, of pity, of rancour. Shame yes, for running away, but that was a momentary impulse, the dregs of a long-lost sense of dignity. In short, sheer languor and weariness of everything, the irresistible urge to bury my head in the sand of my cowardice, these were stronger than any other driving force. Not to mention the spasmodic pangs of toothache that had started up in my mouth and were gnawing away at my mind as well.

This was at first. Then little by little my thoughts went back to the scene witnessed not long ago, first of all to unravel it from the images of *Lancelot*, with which it had somehow become confused and entangled, and thereafter, with more calm and precision, to see the thing instant by instant and relive it in slow motion, like replays of sporting events.

The murdering motorcyclist, a vast bull of a fellow dressed in black leather, had vanished on the instant, and in all honesty I would have been unable to swear to any recognizable features. Besides, was it certain that it was deliberate murder rather than a case of hit and run? And was the blind man really so dangerous that it was worth killing him? When it came down to it, regarding that fatal evening I would be able to furnish only vague hints and approximations: the piazza with the fountain, a bump in the paving, a building with a lot of rooms . . . True, there was the roll of film, but killing its owner did not solve the problem, it meant throwing away the key to its hiding place.

As far as I was concerned, no one knew that I knew the little that I did know, and I couldn't wait to count myself out, going to earth at home again and nursing my submissive expectation of a catastrophe.

It was a brusque awakening, while engrossed in these thoughts, to feel the hand of a gendarme fall heavily on my shoulder. After which, as I have said, my prison life began.

I was not treated as badly as I had feared. In fact, if any faith is to be placed in the motion of gratitude I composed during my wakeful night on a page of a calendar, and left hanging as a souvenir on a nail in my cell wall, the experience was of the win-a-free-holiday type, well suited to a claustrophile such as I am.

Taking as my model the mock-heroic style of Crisafulli, I penned the jotting that word for word I here transcribe:

### In Praise of the *Regina Coeli* prison

*A single room at the Regina Coeli, a snuggery, a garçonnière, with its coenobitic bed and brand-new washbasin, its little blue light forever lit (for the eye also craves its share), is the nearest thing to happiness. Especially if, after walking a whole day on the scorching paving stones of the city, they offer you a free ride in a Black Maria and, spotless as you are, more or less welcome you with a guard of honour, undress you with loving hands, wash you, dress you again in dry cotton garments, put you to bed with the blankets turned down . . . well, Brother Leo, if only the commodities included the Larghetto from K.581 in the background, would this not be perfect bliss?*

*O sweetest warders, mothers and fathers of my choice, my Good Samaritans and shaggy St Bernards! Who could forget the benignant uncouthness of your eye at the spyhole, and how the rims of your fingernails, in the simple gesture of offering a cigarette, manage to include a suggestion of proletarian complicity; who could forget the B flats of your footsteps when mealtime is approaching, or the sand-papering sound of your voices? From you (and I will always remember it) I owe the knowledge of how much more in native freedom does a foot breathe inside a gaping shoe, released from its laces. And also of the fact (I have a notion that one day it will come in useful) that if someone once gets the idea into his head, a shoelace would suffice . . .*

Here, when things were bowling along nicely, my pencil lead broke, and I relapsed into my usual unbearable lucubrations concerning myself. I know that I repeat more or less the same things, but I nourish the hope that if I commit it all to black and white the lost needle will suddenly leap from the haystack, the key to open the strongbox of my secret. Certainly I am forever putting my finger on the same rotten tooth (and not just metaphorically either, with this damned molar torturing my cheek). And yet, to vary the refrain a bit, and to pass from the physical to the moral sphere, I hereby certify once more that the Caucasian eagle to which I give my liver to make a meal of has two heads and two beaks. The first is an insipid bitterness, sceptical of any aim or purpose ("What of it?"); the other is the premonition of suddenly collapsing in the middle of the road and going straight into the dark. A darkness where nothing will count any more, not books or music or memories, not the amorous mewings of Rosa, not certain long-lost, unforgotten midnight lips, not that shimmer of a moon hidden among the magnolias, not the paltry history of men, not the wily smirk of God, not the ruin of the galaxies in the infinite blackness of the remotest skies . . . A black hole where my toothache will cease at last.

Have I made myself clear? No, I have not. It has still to be understood, and I leave it to you to understand, why and how I manage to feel safe inside my recent refuge; how and why at the same time and in all sincerity I persevere in playing the daily game of the humours: moods of anger, of melancholy, and the appetites of the senses . . . how and why I, who am at bottom a mediocre man, nurture within me such a sophistical mixture of clownishness and neurasthenia, using it to master my dominant thought, which is fear (if I have not so far given you to understand this it is for the very reason that I have been afraid to). Fear it is that regulates all my actions. There is not a minute in my day when I am free of the sensation of walking a catwalk half a metre wide between two yawning chasms of nothingness. And it is this word, "nothing", that I find every moment on the tip of my tongue . . . Nothing, nothing, nothing . . . Sometimes I work off steam by filling an entire page of the present diary with these sacred syllables. Then, all of a sudden, confidence restored and self imbued with physical wellbeing, as after a shower or a successful defecation, I turn over a new leaf and start writing *things* again. How can I do otherwise? If in a game one can only lose or cheat, one cheats.

Halfway through the night they unloaded a new client into the cell, a skinny fellow with an extremely sonorous voice, pleasantly drunk. Disturbing the peace at night is the charge, if my diagnosis is correct, followed by resisting the police and picturesque insults directed at all the highest authorities, from the President of the Republic to the President of the Immortals (if I may be forgiven this tiny plagiarism). His entry puts paid to my last scanty hopes of nodding off, already jeopardized by the *lux perpetua* of the blue light above my head, as laid down by the rules and regulations of the place. Worse still when Signor Pecenera (such is his name, ceremoniously announced together with an attempt at a bow), after having with religious zeal filled the pisspot, proceeds to stumble over it, with consequent drenching of himself and oaths scattered to the winds, along with the familiar, unique stench which, gently wafting, is diffused in the air and chastises my nostrils.

What to say, what to do? It's no good, as the saying goes, crying over spilt milk, and I prefer to devote my attention to the newcomer's later effusions, this time purely verbal. Thus I learn that Pecenera, making allowance for his present inebriation, was once a midshipman aboard the good ship *Pharaoh*, sailing the Mediterranean. Times past, the sweet season of youth: a girl in every port, but the best of them all in Genoa, ready to marry him at the next landfall.

At this point, leaving me agape, Pecenera stops talking and falls fast asleep, as if someone has just put a bullet through his brain. Half an hour later, sprightlier than ever, he shakes me by the arm: "What are you doing? Sleeping? Am I boring you?" he asks, moving me to anger or to laughter, it's a toss-up which. His story continues after this fashion, in jerks between one snooze and another, each time picking up exactly where he left off.

Substantially it is the story of the first time he landed up in prison. As a political prisoner, no less, and completely innocent, the victim of a plot. The thing arose – he says – with his being found in possession of a compromising letter from a member of the Red Brigades who had fled the country; but – he swears – he knew nothing about it, it was all a trap set for him by a rival in love who . . .

I don't let him continue. With astonishment and admiration I realize that, with a few updatings, he is telling me the plot of *The Count of Montecristo*.

My interrogation, late the following morning, gets off to a bad start. The inspector mistakes me for someone else, an old jailbird: "Well, look who's here, you scoundrel!"

When he changes his mind (Bendidio has telephoned in the meantime) he apologizes, but his accent, painfully Palermitan, doesn't help him to cultivate the confidingness he hopes for. All the same, I have to hand it to him when he does his level best to assure me that I am not charged with anything, it was just that my sudden disappearance among the crowd caused some perplexity. If they have detained me it is only for the sake of verification and my own protection, in case the murderer – if it is a case of murder – has a mind to rid himself of an eyewitness. But it seems that this is not the case, and they wish me God-speed, after getting me to draw (smile, please) an identikit of the culprit, practically no more than a crash-helmet, a leather jacket and gloves, like millions of others in the world.

Reaching home, I find my room invaded. It is Cesare begging my hospitality for the night. The police have not allowed a wake, and have put seals on the apartment. It appears they are still investigating Tir's death, even if half-heartedly. Indeed, in my own statement I said that the motorcyclist seemed more in the grip of a frenzy rather than prompted by a deliberate intention, but plainly no one believed that the accident was fortuitous. It was probable even that between the two deaths, of Ersilia and of Tir, some would-be Maigret had already sniffed out a link, a tie-up.

In the upshot it was two policemen who kept watch over the body. They were scarcely persuaded to allow Cesare to put a bunch of flowers in the coffin, and also (as had been Tir's wish) the Kodak Brownie that had been scarcely more than a toy, but his first equipment as an amateur photographer. The funeral has been fixed for late tomorrow, in the hope that Matilde, finally traced to some Mediterranean beach or other, can get back in time for it.

This Cesare tells me while he undresses and gets ready to sleep on a pallet on the floor.

Once the light is out I have an intense longing to immure myself and my worries in the sepulchre of slumber: too many emotions in the last few hours, and too many hours without sleep. But Cesare seems to disagree with me, he is full to the brim and needs somewhere to pour it all out:

"What will become of me now that Signor Bartolo is dead? I don't have a home or a family, and I've only got half a trade. I'm in for a tough time . . . "

"There's always Matilde," I suggest, not without malice.

"O *her!*" and his voice breaks with the sorrow of it. In the darkness I hear a soft gasp, as of someone gulping down both air and tears. I make no effort to push that matter further, it's as plain as a pikestaff that the lad was used for twenty-four hours and then discarded. Besides, I am more impelled by a sleuthlike curiosity:

"How did it happen, that evening? Why didn't Tir take you with him?"

"The clients came to pick him up in a car, they wanted just him. I saw them start out for I don't know where, and four hours later come back I don't know where from. That's what I told the Inspector, and it's all I know."

A minute later (ah, the blessings of youth!) I hear him snoring: the hearty, vigorous note of an engine destined to last, afflicted by few memories. Whereas mine . . .

And once again, like yesterday, while I lie stretched out near someone else's sleeping body, I count over and over the interminable sheep of my interminable night in Gethsemane.

# NINE

# The Funeral

*Saturday, August 26th*

Funeral processions almost never fail to suggest an outing and a charade. You can see from a mile off that the mourners, even if they are rending their garments, are bursting with relief at being alive and at their crushing superiority over the dear departed. To that is added the vanity of feeling themselves actors not in the trite comedy of every day, but in an event of tragic stamp. Playing second lead this time around, while waiting to become, some day or other, the mute protagonists.

Such behaviour is more in evidence than ever in the present case, in which Tir's bier is followed by a swarm of fellow tenants and acquaintances. Of real friends there is no one except me, unemotional by nature and philosophy; of his relatives only his sister, just arrived and still in her travelling clothes, and from her I scarcely expected copious tears. Otherwise the only one missing is Lo Surdo, who is in detention but soon, they say, will be granted house-arrest. Present, however, are trumpeter Bisceglie, Leah, Mariposa in stiletto heels, a representative of the Association for the Blind, the two Greeks with their offspring, and everyone else from the building. Even Mundula has put himself out, looking just adequately sad, and is walking side by side with Pirzio Ravalli (God knows what they have to talk about). No possible doubt, however, about the conversation going on in front of me between

Donna Marzia and the fortune-teller, in voices louder than the occasion warrants. The mourning-squad pays little attention to them, but, being right on their heels, how can I avoid it?

"I am worried about my son," says Adriana. "He's one of those who love to destroy things. For the moment he is sparing his fellow men, thank goodness, but everything that has wings, tail or claws, everything that yelps, crawls, mews or flies, gets on his nerves. It's all right if he kills ants, flies and cockroaches in the kitchen, it helps to keep the house clean, but when it comes to pigeons, sparrows and cats, I ask you why?"

"It's the television that encourages monsters like that," Donna Marzia replies with a shudder. Her voice is gentle and low, and emerges by way of a wrinkled dewlap like an Alpine rivulet flowing through furrows and ditches; a voice that in every cadence evokes olden-day balls in the garden, bare shoulders, elbow-length gloves, fans, jewels, kisses stolen on the veranda in the shelter of a rose espalier . . .

Donna Marzia, as I have already mentioned, is an old lady who survives by occasionally selling some family picture or print. I have several times noticed black-clad dealers coming down the stairs, under their arms a canvas or portfolio, something of greater or lesser value. Another remnant of the noble lady's erstwhile opulence is a large black marble chapel in the Campo Verano cemetery, and it is there that Tir's remains will provisionally rest, until a permanent place becomes available.

"Maurizio," continues his mother, "worries the life out of me. Look at him there, how brazenly he's mimicking Signora Garaffa, with the two twins laughing their heads off. They've got too fond of him, much too fond. They stick as close to his sides as two policemen to a prisoner. And he has rings under his eyes and a neck that's got too scrawny for his shirt-collar. I don't want to think evil . . . "

"It's his age," chirrups the noble, adorable octogenarian, who never budges an inch from the obvious, but with such heraldic grace as to elevate platitudes into assertions of timeless wisdom.

At this point the procession is joined by a stranger: flowing locks down to his shoulders, ear-ring in his left ear, freakish slogans on his jeans-jacket. In short a cross between a disc-jockey and a ladies' hairdresser. What's he doing here? Could be because I've got a guilty conscience, but I definitely feel under surveillance, I see shadows and spies everywhere. Naturally my mind is awhirl with the vanished roll of film (from now on, VR for short). God knows where it is hidden, Tir can't have breathed a word about it to anyone, I'm probably the only person to know of its existence. Except, I fear, the interested parties . . .

Overtaking more sedate mourners, Crisafulli catches up with me, falls in step and takes my arm: "Poor Bartolo, what a shame. And to think I had a part for him in my play the day after tomorrow . . . " He begins telling me about it, but his voice reaches my ears like the drone of distant bees. He notices this: "Where are you keeping your head nowadays?" "Elsewhere," I reply with a vague gesture. I can scarcely tell him that I am mentally picturing what the shots on VR would reveal to me, if I could manage to find it. But even more intensely I imagine the sequel, after Tir's departure: the fun and games are over, the revellers lie exhausted on the beds, the tables, the floor. The first light of dawn showing greyly in the windows and on the tiles, along with the usual litter of fag-ends, corks, syringes and assorted leftovers of lovemaking, reveals an unexpected corpse, perhaps an OD case. Everyone is seized by panic, until the most decisive of those present makes up his mind for all of them: clean the place up completely, dump the still-stoned Dorotea somewhere or other, abandon Ersilia's body in a distant doorway, and all will be well. Then they remember the photographs. Thank

God the photographer was blind, and they have the negatives. Then the suspicion: all of them? They count, and suspicion becomes a certainty: one is missing. So they hire a muscle-man, Tir is killed and all around him is scorched earth. But what about me? They have seen me sitting next to him in the cinema, they have seen me with him when he died . . . Am I too in danger of my life?

I shut my eyes and recapture that leather-clad thug, the pitiless determination with which he aimed straight for the blind man and mangled him. An accident? An execution? At this point I ought to . . . I ought to, but once more I plummet into one of those states of absolute catatonia that recur in my life. Like the day when the beggar was dying in the snow outside my window, and I stood there watching him, watching him, watching him . . .

"Try with cod-liver oil. In my day it worked miracles," says Donna Marzia, but Adriana shakes her head and puts a finger to her lips: we are passing a church. Matilde starts sobbing even more loudly, while continuously running her palms over her hips to smooth out the wrinkles in her long skirt. A strange young person, whom I imagine quick to orgasm in both body and heart.

It is quite some way to the cemetery, and the cortège breaks up and re-forms in a different order; so that, to speak only of myself, I find myself now beside, now behind and now in front of each of the mourners, according to the undulatory progress of the procession.

O sea, an everlasting rebeginning . . .

comes to my lips of its own accord: another variant to add to the catalogue in my translation notebook. Very deep rooted in me is the habit (or vice) of subjecting life and letters to a perpetual ballot; mine is a duplex heart, and I relapse even in situations like

today's, which calls for gravity and compassion. Even worse: since
I'm still in the mood for analogies, and having a small but heterogeneous company at my disposal, I mentally try subjecting it to
my favourite test and sport, which is to identify each of those
present with a personage known to me, whether in a novel, a play
or a film. At one time, when I used to travel, I would do the same
with landscapes, but since I've been living in a suburban area and
never leave it, once having decided that it's a third-rate dump of
a place, the game is over. With people of flesh and blood, on the
other hand, the possibilities are far more ample and prolific. For
every ten times that the pairing seems too outlandish for words,
one time it miraculously comes off, producing an amalgam
between reality and invention that enriches my sense of both the
one and the other. To cite the simplest example, Lo Surdo, or *The
Reluctant Mafioso*, would be quite at home in a novel by some
would-be Sciascia, while the others pose more problems. Though
Tir, poor fellow, could easily put himself on the waiting list
for a remake of the *Storia dell'occhio*; Leah and her father-
stepfather-godfather would make a good couple in one of Ivy
Compton-Burnett's families; Mundula . . . here (though I am
flattering him) it is not an author but an actor who comes to my
aid. I am thinking of Jules Berry, an ignoble but sorrowful charla-
tan and ham of the 1930s. As for me, I see myself (let's set our
sights high) halfway between Krapp of the Last Tape and one of
Tommaso Landolfi's spinsters, though not without the disappointed urge to impersonate one of Robert Walser's servile heroes.
But I continue with my inspection, and examining the backs ahead
of me I am arrested by Pirzio Ravalli and at him I bog down, to
such an extent does he seem to oscillate between a city-maddened
man and a crafty "mole". I would say Le Carré, if I weren't afraid of
loading too much weight on his shoulders: it's a malady of mine,
to want to see a well where there's only a rush-hidden puddle.

I admit that my impressions regarding the mystery of this man, confused as they are, agree on one point: that it's a tricky one. It's not that I am at all costs trying to inject a thrill of adventure into our humdrum tenants' co-operative, but I would not be surprised if we discovered that he is a drug peddler or spy or escaped convict. Or else a collaborator with justice, under police protection without our knowing it. Certainly he is hiding something. You only have to see how he walks hugging the walls, a fierce light in his downcast eyes, with a bulging bag slung round his neck, which, if it does not hold a time-bomb, at least conceals a revolver. And if, eavesdropping behind him while in conversation with Mundula, I have caught only perfectly innocent phrases, that concern nothing more sinister than marking by zones or individual players in the game of football, I am reassured only for a moment, just time to become convinced that those words contain some treacherous metaphor. To make a précis of the portrait of him I have in mind, and must remember to transcribe into my notebook, here it is: about thirty-five, on the ugly side, protruding nose and chin, eyes – when visible at all – like two muddy puddles; cheeks the colour of asphalt; narrow brow, barrack-room haircut, and taken all in all more a gasmask than a face.

Modes of behaviour: cordiality for a moment on meeting; thereafter a brusque recoil, a guardedness that comes down like a steel shutter, rather like those maps of Africa on which ancient cartographers showed the coastlines but hid the lions.

What papers does he buy? Nothing but cars, sport and gossip. Am I going too far in suspecting that he doesn't read them, but buys them only as red herrings? However that may be I decide to sound him out, to force him willy-nilly to spit out a few words: "Do you play chess?" I enquire of him. And when he nods: "Would you like a game with me?"

"I don't have the time, alas."

"We could do it by correspondence, a move a day."

"By correspondence?"

"Well, not by post, of course. We could tell each other our moves on the intercom. It would only take a minute."

"A strange choice, for two people living in the same building."

"You know, faced with someone in person I get too easily worked up. I prefer challenges at a distance, with an invisible enemy."

He smiles, and then in sugared tones: "Forgive me, dear fellow, I was simply showing off. I can't play chess."

*Touché*. Rather than Le Carré, his prototype is in someone more like Dürrenmatt.

Here comes our jazz fiend Bisceglie, a cheerful youngster with fair hair and a goatee like Dizzy Gillespie's. But he also lives clean, he doesn't drink or sniff or womanize. Occasionally he invites me up to listen to some disc or other he's found at the Ricordi bargain counter. I'm sorry to say it, but he couldn't care less about Tir's death, for him this funeral is simply an outing, an excuse for a change of air.

"I've picked up 'Relaxin' at Camarillo'. You know," he explains, "the one that goes *Ta-kata-ta takatakakata-ta* . . . "

I must admit that his passion for Charlie Parker leaves me cold. Always the same tortuous laments from entrails riddled with carrion cancer. Beautiful stuff, there's no denying it. But to my mind, if I'm going to have music, I want it to be a seraphic massage soothing the scars of the soul. Or at the most, pure pandemonium with a riot of pyrotechnics and one hell of a hullabaloo. But anyway, Johnnie slips an arm into mine, murmurs that he hasn't got a bean and is afraid they'll evict him. And he chooses to tell this to me, more penniless even than he is. "Have you got any friends?" I ask him. "Someone who would give you a bed?"

"There's the garage where we rehearse, I'll get by. After all," and it's as if he were waving under my nose a credit card valid for all time. "I'm only twenty . . . "

Now we are at the gates, the hearse pulls up for the usual formalities: unloading the baggage, signing in, getting a room number . . . And there we have Tir set up for eternity, stiff and stinking, withering, cold as any stone, four hard planks for his resting place. I think of the dark glasses we left over his eyes. I think of the little box camera that Cesare forced into his hands, along with rosary beads with a Latin cross. They'll both come in handy at the hour of resurrection, if he's reborn with two good eyes and it's a sunny day.

It's Matilde who insisted on us following on foot, as they used to in the old days wherever she came from. The modern way would be a far quicker business, no sooner dead than buried: five minutes in church, a hearse at full tilt, a De Profundis and home we go. We all agreed with her, partly so as not to go against her wishes, partly to stretch our legs a bit by parading solemnly through the city, as synchronized as chorus girls at the Ambra Jovinelli. It will be a perk for our anonymous, extinct identities; a way of making a group and a family of us, disunited and root-less as we are. I in particular, though devoted to my solitude, am very grateful for the fact that in an appointed place, and sharing such problems as gas, water, telephones and television aerials, a miniature community surrounds me with some warmth, someone I can run to in case of tummyache or heartbreak, someone to catch on the landing and exchange a few words with about the rain or the fine weather . . . Doors to knock at, hands to shake on New Year's Day, a cheap and harmless sample of swarming, hostile humanity. Here I can look about me fearlessly, all passion spent. So it comes about that now, as

Tir's friend, I can easily resign myself to his death; infatuated with Leah, I am ready to trade her image for any other worthy substitute. I mean that, *pro domo mea*, I have learnt the prudence and astuteness of meting out all my emotions with a view to economy: like putting the car into neutral for a long downhill stretch. Only this keeps me from shoving my head in a noose. Once upon a time my nerves were sheepdogs, baying at every full moon. Now, if I haven't exactly pensioned them off, at least I've laid them off temporarily. I've thinned down my life, and the pain along with it. I am mine own usurer, I demand from myself exorbitant interest rates that only I can pay. At the same time exploiter and exploited, from this reciprocal swindle I derive a calm, angelic satisfaction . . .

Have I been boring you? Bear with me for another minute and I'll have finished. For when it comes to understanding myself I really do set about it from every angle and never give up. Why, a kitten playing with a ball of wool would give up sooner than I do. I know of no alternative, it's so alluring to heal myself by writing. At the risk, clumsy Luddite that I am, of blowing up the whole works of the novel . . .

Having deposited Tiresias in his silent, everlasting blindness, we make our way homewards at random, in scattered groups. Some wait at the bus-stop while the more affluent look for a taxi. Only a handful of us are left on foot: myself, Johnnie, the philosopher and Crisafulli, which is to say one youngster, one man of middle age and two ripe in years, so that the former pair falls in with the adagio of the latter. A funeral pace, therefore, as on the way there; and one favourable to conversation. As the one best off for breath it is the trumpeter who speaks first:

"Tommaso," says he, "d'you remember that Jelly Roll Morton I played you on Sunday, 'Dead Man Blues'?"

I don't encourage him, out of the corner of my eye I've seen that fifty yards behind, on Shanks's pony like the rest of us, the man with the ear-ring is following. I wonder if he is simply going the same way or is shadowing us . . .

Bisceglie persists: "It's only the blacks who know how to celebrate death." And quite undaunted he begins to whistle the tune, until he sees Crisafulli's face snap shut like an umbrella.

It's Placido who saves the situation: "The blacks, you say? Well certainly those lively marches of theirs, when they come back from the cemetery at the double . . . It's the right way to get used to the idea. Much as the Mexican Indians do with their sweetmeats in the shape of skeletons."

Crisafulli relaxes: "When I think that thanks to drugs we shall all become immortal . . . "

"With luck," is Bisceglie's naïve rejoinder, but Crisafulli follows up with, "On the contrary, God forbid. It's just as well we still have suicide. It's the subject of the one-acter I'm shortly going to present to you."

As we say nothing so as not to egg him on, he continues: "It's called *The Filibuster* and is set in Parliament, at Montecitorio."

In the meanwhile Ear-ring has drawn almost level, he is practically poised to overtake. That's not the technique if you're tailing someone, perhaps I've made an overhasty judgement. Is he some unknown friend of the deceased, or just a collector of funerals? We only need to ask him, and so I do as soon as he draws abreast of us: "Hey, you!"

He has been wishing for nothing better than to join us, and a moment later we already know all about him. He is an old colleague and partner of Tir's, in times when Tir still had his sight, and that's all there is to it. A photographer himself, a specialist in late-night discotheques, hence the get-up, though unseemly, he admits, for his age. He read the news in the "Spyglass" (my heart gives a leap: it used to be my paper) and felt it beholden on him etc., etc. He had even bought a bunch of flowers but lost it on the way. However, to be absolutely frank, he would not have come without a specific purpose, which is to talk to the heirs about an idea of his: on his own or in partnership with Tir's sister, to take over the firm, equipment, archives, address books, and carry the business on. He would pay the proper price, needless to say. In any case, now that Tir is dead what use is his professional clobber to anyone else? To that snotty-nosed assistant of his? He doubts it. He sounds convincing enough. All the same I'd dearly like to hear what Cesare has to say on the subject, were it not for the fact that the lad left at dawn, right after his cup of coffee, and hasn't even come to the ceremony. Between him and Matilde yesterday, in the fleeting moments when their eyes met, there were stony looks on sullen faces that might have been immobilized by plastic surgery. However, I explain to Signor Camillo (for such is his name, if we are to credit him) it is Matilde and she alone who can decide the matter, for we are mere acquaintances and sympathizers.

"Be that as it may," he replies, "I can't find her. Where is she?"

The philosopher, pompous as ever, though not without a sting of irony: "I have not seen her since the service. Vanished, ascended into heaven! *Et in coelum exiluit*, like an ancient king of Rome."

Camillo gives him a sidelong glance and then, at full tilt as it were, also vanishes into thin air.

As for us, step by step, here we are home at last. With a surprise awaiting us: the seals on Tir's apartment have been broken and the place has been turned upside down.

It's young Maurizio who brings us these tidings, in tones so brimful of joy that he might be the archangel Gabriel on a mission to the Virgin Mary. He it was, he boasts, who made the discovery when the thieves were still inside, on account of a damaged seal which led him to suspect it had been tampered with. A shame that he wasted time trying to recruit the twins as allies and took the trouble to arm himself with his famous mouse-slaying catapult. Otherwise he would have caught them red-handed. He has stayed on guard, but he fears the stable is empty, the horse has bolted, the loot has vanished.

What loot? I wonder. Could it not be VR, that humble roll of film worth a win on the pools, which presumably portrays all the dirtiest brazen faces of the capital? A snatch devoutly to be wished, but how come the police failed to find it when they searched the flat before? Unless they did find it, and suppressed it in the interests of national self-respect (anything is possible, and far worse happens on the Telly).

A gentle shove at the door and it gives way like a paper screen. The others follow gingerly. The hallway is in darkness, but I flick on all the lights and am through the three-bedroom place in a matter of seconds. It is an utter shambles. The one and only thing in all the havoc, with the contents of every piece of furniture or object whatever strewn over the floor, including the goldfish from the smashed aquarium (God rest its soul), the bottles from the medicine chest, the springs from the prewar leather armchair, the tatters of a fake De Pisis (an old birthday present from me), the secrets of the secrétaire . . . the one and only thing to remain intact in its bellicose, upright, English imperturbability, is a white stick in the umbrella rack.

# TEN

# Manoeuvres, Agitations, Negotiations

*Friday, September 1st*

When I began these pages I imagined I would be writing the diary of an isolation, such as those kept by certain researchers, record-holders at survival, who let themselves down into a pothole where they live without awareness of time. I find myself, on the contrary, having to relate a jumble of events as dense as it is dynamic. And not only to relate these but, alas, to partake of them in the first person, if only as a little cog-wheel forced to turn in unison with the mechanism as a whole. I remember a witticism I thought up at the start of my experiment, describing myself as a Crusoe minus not only Man Friday but any Friday whatsoever. I now realize that the joke has to be annulled, not only regarding the swank of making myself out a half-wit, since in fact I have never felt so reasonable and master of myself, but in the other respect, the illusion of being alone on an island, since my modest lodging has become a port of call for all comers, and not five minutes goes by but an imperious pummelling at the door noisily arouses me (for some days now, clean contrary to my habits, I have been double- or treble-locking myself in).

At this very moment, knock, knock, knock, here we go again. It is a profusely sweating messenger, an old acquaintance from the "Spyglass", who stands in the doorway and bids me good morning. "Bollocks", as we used to call him in the newsroom on account of his abuse of this expletive in his frugal discourses, is a man stalwart of limb and simple of mind, employed by the paper for the most laborious and elementary tasks. As on this occasion to deliver a message by hand, in default of telephone or fax, to the above-mentioned addressee in the person of yours truly, Tommaso Mulè. "It's from the Editor," he mumbles, and stands there waiting for a tip and an answer, far from supposing that neither is on the agenda.

The message reads: "Tommaso, how are you? What's it like to be a free man again? I expected a word of thanks, but it never came. Here at the paper it's the same old life: spites and jealousies, scoops that come off, or don't, or are invented: bizarre crimes, interviews with Tom, Dick and Harry M.P., and trying every time to pass our howlers off as misprints . . . In short, business as usual, as when you were here. I won't tell you we miss you because I'd be lying. After all, you wanted to leave as much as I wanted you to. An admirable convergence of views, which enables me to hope that you don't hold anything against me. It now chances that you, busy they tell me rewriting a Barbellion or an Amiel in a below-stairs lair for spiders; it chances, I repeat, that you find yourself living in the succulent heart of a Story, with a capital S. Witness to a presumed murder, friend of the presumed victim, in the know (we gather) about his secrets, well acquainted with the places and people involved, already on the spot . . . Well, what would you say to coming back to us as Special Crime Correspondent? Don't refuse at once, wait until we have ten minutes' chat. It's a bigger thing than you think. For you, if you refuse, there's only danger, whereas if you accept there is danger and money. I beg you to answer with a yes or no. Bollocks is standing there waiting."

"No," I snap at the man, taking him aback. "No," I repeat when he sketches a protesting gesture, indeed with both hands I urge him gently out of the door. When he is already on his way and I see his long legs passing before my spyhole, I have belated second thoughts and bellow out "Bollocks! Bollocks!", scandalizing the passers-by who hear such an indelicate utterance issuing from those Acherontic depths. I rush out and catch up with him under the awning of the "Minibar" across the road. "I've thought again," I gabble at him. "Villa Borghese gardens at three this afternoon. The Valle Giulia entrance. Meanwhile take him this." And I hand him my account of the Lo Surdo affair.

I have in fact thought again. It's pointless to kid myself, I've been swept up in the dance so I might as well keep in time with the music. My father taught me that when a fish is hooked and as good as done for it might as well swallow the bait. Fierce tantrums from my mother at that time, she being understandably convinced that this proverb concealed an envenomed allusion to herself and their marriage. The truth is that Bendidio has hit the nail on the head. To do as I have done so far, seeking happiness in indolence, could work for me only as long as I was alone, but when it's a whole people on the move it's not so much a flight as an exodus. What use is it to swim against the tide? I fooled myself into thinking I was marking time in the midst of a surging mob, eluding the authority of computers, entropies, holes in the ozone. Unresigned to the velocity of history; furious at having in the course of a few decades to scrap my pianola cylinders for 78s, those for long-players, those again for compact disks, and yet again for supercompacts (all Beethoven's Nine in a few centimetres, the devil take them!); presuming to measure time and my own life by the imperceptible tempo of drips in a cavern of stalactites. And behold me, on the contrary, press-ganged into the cast of an off-peak-hour television script, under the impression of not really seeing the action at all, but being manoeuvred by it, as happens to all extras on the small screen; but in the certainty that in a saraband so thronged with figures both he and she, it is inevitable that with his only-too-familiar suite of sighs and blood, death will sooner or later lead the dance. A return, I tell myself – and here Bendidio is right – that could touch me closely, so that to have a word with him, to understand what quicksand I am sinking into, is not a bad idea. What's more, if he prints and pays for *In Actual Fact*, it's all grist to my mill.

I used to come to the park at Villa Borghese with Rosa at the time when I was courting her. I remember hours of drowsy and tender monotony, with children playing ball and losing it in the bushes, then coming rushing out because they've been scared by a lizard; feverishly excited corporals in full seduction-gear conversing with baby-sitters, while they dry the wet paint on the bench with the seat of their pants. Around us the gentle sounds of water and sunlight: yes, sounds of sunlight, because in its sparkle, already attenuated by the first nipping airs of September, one seems to hear a muted crackle, as of sparks in a cooling crucible. But the solitary swan swimming on the lake no longer arouses thoughts in me, as once it did.

I find Bendidio a good deal plumper, with short socks inside his tiny moccasins, as grubby as ever and as ever full of insults and blandishments together. He comes to the point at once: I will have seen that we are in all the papers. It is becoming increasingly obvious that Tir's accident was no accident; that Ersilia Trapani, poor child, with her metal brace on her teeth, was found to have several gallons too much crack in her veins; that her companion Dorotea was found at dawn astride the wall of

the Tiber Embankment, glassy-eyed and empty-minded, unable
to say where she had been or whom she had consorted with in
the last seventy-two hours. But just lucid enough to remember
posing for a blind photographer. This link once found, the
investigation has been steaming ahead and I, as Tir's friend and
presumed depository of his confidences, am in it up to the neck.
No accusations so far, but don't I see that it's in my own best
interests to bring the matter to light? So why don't I write for
the "Spyglass", as in the old days, clearing my name and at the
same time working for truth and justice?

Here Bendidio's voice, like an over-revved engine, begins
to misfire, and his solemn peroration starts to seep away into
shallows and marshes, like the Po at its delta. When he gets
into his stride again the gist of his proposals is as follows: since
everyone is looking for VR, which would fill in the blanks in
the crossword, the important thing is to find it, reveal the identity
of the protagonists and nail them with the pictorial evidence.
There are already whispers as to who they are, but a shortage of
proofs. Rumours are circulating about a gang unimaginatively
dubbed "The Druggists", who sell drugs as well as taking them
at exclusive parties. The ringleader is said to be a woman known
as La Badalona, of practically royal blood, now sullied by plebeian
vices, at one time the queen of the salons in fashionable Parioli
and now the procuress of the most forbidden pleasures. She
suffers, it would appear, from a particular obsession: she is not
convinced that a single darned thing has truly happened or been
enjoyed unless she has a record of it and can reproduce it. Hence
her legendary collection of rare, indeed unique items to put all
other such collections in the shade: from a bound and helpless
Mr Spartacus '92 being raped by Lady D. to the flash of His
Eminence Cardinal Z. seated practically naked on the lap of
a seminarist. How does she work it? She hires half-starved

paparazzi, pays them by the reel but always keeps the negatives herself, and then (here's the laugh!) she plays them back to the subjects themselves for a few million in subscription fees. It's a kind of club, you see?

Until this present hitch, with two country girls lured in, ill-used and dumped. You can imagine the rest, what is not yet known but ought to be known, and above all proved.

Thus did Bendidio half speak, half mumble, finally producing a post-dated cheque made out to me: "This is for *The Case of the Blind Photographer*, when you have written it. We'll see about *In Actual Fact* when the time comes."

What should I say? The offer attracts and repels me in equal measure. In any case, if only to raise my price, I say no. And he, without ceasing to be rude, adopts a note of entreaty: "Tommaso, you are a half-wit, on that I have never had any doubts. But I like you all the more for it, and that's why I'm asking you for help. You used to write under this masthead, didn't you? You can't have forgotten it: *semel abbas, semper abbas*. So do it for the paper's sake, or call it *esprit de corps,* call it patriotism. Because, well . . . you want to know why? The fact is, if we don't get in a blow under the belt at this point, something to double our circulation, we'll have to shut up shop. You simply can't let down your old colleagues – hey, what am I saying: your brethren! And there's more to it than that. Think of the readers, of what they'll lose, of the thousand million watts of truth that are extinguished with the death of a newspaper. When, late in the evening, I spy the newsroom from my glass cubicle, and all those heads bent over keyboards grinding out fragments of truth, and then I open my windows and lean out over Piazza Esedra and all its floodlights, and I think of the throngs, the multitudes (well, fewer now than formerly but still a lot of people) who go to bed happy because they know that tomorrow with the milk they will receive a copy of the 'Spyglass'; when I listen to the presses rolling out column after column of messages to the universe, ah, what can I say? I am touched, I am moved, I get a lump in my throat. And now must that lighthouse be darkened, that great orchestra fall silent? All because of a few photos that cannot be found? While if we had them in our hands they would be like a crutch to us, we would have our rivals cornered, the 'Pen of the Year Prize' would be ours for sure . . . ."

I tore up the cheque, told him I'd do it but demanded cash – little, blighted, but on the nail. I'd use it to buy a coffee-machine and a new portable typewriter. I'd give Leah Buozzi a bunch of orchids or chrysanthemums . . .

I had not exchanged so much as a nod with Leah since we last met. I am now counting on seeing her this evening at the tenants' meeting, which promises some excitement for many reasons. Meanwhile I dwell on what to do regarding the first steps in my investigation; or rather, I decide to dwell on them without having a chance to put my decision into effect. I had better explain myself. I am a mental lazybones and reflection is only possible to me under certain conditions of a ceremonial order, as with some people in the business of getting to sleep. In my case I need to be lying on my back on the bed, my head resting on a low pillow, in one of my hands a clip-board with a blank sheet of paper, in the other a biro, to enable me to give immediate written substance to the birds of thought which flit through my mind and would otherwise be off and away. That is what I intend to do this time, but at the very moment I am putting the key in the lock the din of many voices and footsteps in the adjacent hallway stays my hand. I go back up the few steps, poke my head round the corner. A small party is on the move, with Mundula lording it over them, haughty and categorical, a boss to his fingertips. At his heels come zealots bearing engineering equipment. It slowly dawns on me (I have heard a rumour about it) that this must be the Commission of Experts sent by the Civil Engineering Department to verify the solidity of the building. Snippets of conversation reach my ears: "What about the Leaning Tower of Pisa?", "Would a steel girder help?", "Someone's trying it on here", "Walls that would withstand a giant earthquake", and suchlike. A reassuring diagnosis, but for the fact that I, concealed by the panel of letterboxes, witness between Mundula and the senior member of the team, both of whom have hung back from the rest, a furtive handshake and a mutual smile of triumph which alone would suffice to accuse them of fraud. Anyway, not even I am convinced that we are running any serious risks, and Garaffa's apprehensions still seem to me a midsummer night's dream. I have other things on my mind, and couldn't care less as I watch all five squeeze into the lift without a thought as to how many it will carry.

When they are out of sight I return to my lair. It has become a sheath, a womb, this beggarly abode of mine. Cooler, moreover, than any other room in the building: something not to be sneezed at in these days when the city is sizzling like a snail on hot coals. I therefore carry on as planned, undressing, stretching out on the bed and staring at the ceiling. I have drawn the flimsy curtains over my window so as to suffer no distractions, and through them percolates a milky, chlorotic light propitious to thought while sufficient for note-taking. Three in number are the cruel crosses to which I feel nailed: the mystery of VR and the murder of poor Tir; the double threat hanging over me, from the police as well as the mysterious "druggists", both convinced that I know something I don't: and my feelings, alternately tepid and seething, for Leah. Three crosses which I mark down on paper and label in Greek style as Pathos, Phobos and Eros, partly to lend them dignity, partly to baffle any spying eyes. On the first point I think of my lost friend for five distressful minutes, then put it aside and pass on to the second. Here there are only two possibilities: either the gang which ransacked Tir's flat succeeded in finding VR, in whichcase I have nothing more to fear, or the search was unfruitful and I'm in trouble. I worry less about the police, for they must be fed up with pestering me. In any case time will tell. I can only hope to come through safely and at the same time, finding myself in the thick of it, to try and match up to Bendidio's expectations.

As for the third cross, you can call it that again! I love you – or something like it – voluptuous Leah! I have only to think of you and you stand before me, I have you in my very eyes, a waxen image of the infant Jesus, except for the profane superabundance of your breasts, seeing which, and guessing at the texture of their flesh, gives me pins and needles in my hands, or at least the wish to clap them . . . An angel painted by Serpotta, whose milk-white nudity it comes naturally to lust after between two milk-white sheets, and with a shudder of guilt approaching that of an anatomist tempted by the limbs of a corpse. In this, I have realized, consists her secret: in the marriage of ice and lava, of hidden fire beneath a veil of most diaphanous alabaster. It occurs to me that even her name sounds inappropriate. Not Leah should she be called, but Lorelei, Ophelia, Ulalume, names of drowned women, of water-ghosts met with only in libraries . . .

Stop! This time I have left the door ajar and the miracle happens. Leah enters without knocking and without a word hastily undresses at my bedside. All this obviously makes no sense at all, and my first impulse is to do a Doubting Thomas and prod her with a forefinger. But at once her voice, throaty and mellow, assures me she is real:

"I've come to sell myself. My price is the roll of film. Otherwise I'll get dressed and there's an end to it."

My look is one of mingled fear and astonishment: she is marmoreal-beautiful-touchable at my side, but as things stand more remote than Fujiyama. To begin with, shopping for eroticism has never been my way, I wilt immediately. Secondly and conclusively, the price she is asking is impossible, I have no idea where the goods in question are to be found. This I tell her, absurdly stiff and decorous, my mouth but inches from her own. She stands up, dons the few scraps of clothing she came in and moves majestically to the door. There she turns and says: "Would you care to look for it for me? For me it's a matter of life or death. I was at that party too."

And off she goes without another word.

I spend an hour in cogitation, soaking in the tub which serves me as bath and think-tank. The cold water tautens both skin and grey matter. Eventually I get a brainwave: if I have to face an adventure I might as well go the whole hog. I get dressed, leave the building, and from the bar across the road I call up Bendidio. I ask for the address of La Badalona. "What d'you want it for?" "That's my business, you just give it me and if I don't ring back within six hours call the police."

Armed with the information I mount Cesare's bicycle, which has been garaged with me, and off I set. Needless to say the palazzo is an ancient one in an ancient piazza. I'd have betted anything on a fountain in the middle, remembering Tir's description, but there isn't one and it's a big disappointment. I also try walking about a bit, feeling for bumps in the paving. Nothing doing, it's all smooth, polished, like a freshly shaven chin. What of it? That doesn't stop me, the main door is open and in I go. But seeing a man of saddle and cycle-clips the porter is filled with indignation.

"Where do you think you're going?"

I plead an interview of great urgency, confidential reasons. At last I persuade him to call upstairs on the intercom. Strangely enough there is no difficulty, the pass is granted.

On entering, though, I find a surprise awaiting me. The door is opened not by a butler or footman. Still less am I welcomed by the lady of the house, whose intimidating features and epic nose worthy of a warrior queen I know from the newspapers, but by an apparently mindless girl, presumably the daughter, who smiles but says nothing. I gaze around me. Lord alive what a lofty ceiling, what opera-house-sized chandeliers, and on the walls what sexy pastels by Rosalba Carriera. Simply to walk the narrow marble pathway between one Bukhara rug and the next makes me feel as out of place as a dung-beetle on a camellia. The girl goes on smiling as I step towards her. A fringe, a touch of make-up, she looks fresh out of boarding school. Only her perfume, circumspect but with a trace of impudence, betrays a whorish streak in her.

"Mother darling is not at home," she murmurs in a voice that if you could put a colour to it would be blue. It doesn't take much to realize she's full of acid from the roots of her hair to the tips of her toes.

"What's your name?" she asks, swaying precariously and clutching at my arm for support. I don't know what instinctive jest or pretence at identification makes me introduce myself as the late lamented "Mattia Pascal", but she doesn't bat an eyelid. It must be the first time she has ever come across the name.

Still clinging to me, with gentle insistence she coaxes me to the sofa, takes a seat beside me, laughs for no reason and interrogates me frivolously: "What do you want? Where have you sprung from? Have we been to bed together? Your face is not unfamiliar." And in the meantime she explores with a finger between the first and second buttons of my shirt, stroking my eyelids with her other, ring-laden hand, the nails bitten down to the quick.

I wouldn't have a clue what to do but for the entry at this moment of a sort of governess in para-military nurse's uniform. Edgy, anxious, and without a word to me, she swoops down on the girl and uproots her from me, heaving at her arm with all the delicacy of a pair of dental forceps. The girl scarcely has time to blow me a kiss before she goes limp and allows herself to be led away without a struggle. I am left alone, nonplussed, but determined to stay put. In the course of a few minutes I receive several visits in quick succession: an oriental manservant with minute features and kindly eyes; a second round with the governess; finally a demoniac in metal-worker's overalls much too small for him. All three advise me to hop it, there's no telling when their mistress will be back or if she will wish to see me, so why not come back tomorrow? None of them insist in the face of my obstinacy: "I'll wait. I have grave matters to communicate. Your employer will not punish you."

An hour goes by. Like a public speaker waiting to take the platform I run over the spiel I have learnt by heart. Impudent it may be, but perhaps the thing to get me out of my present fix, or at least to learn a little more about it. In the meantime I step cautiously around the grand room, careful not to wreak havoc amongst all that precious crystal and those smooching couples from Sèvres. My attention is caught by an album lying on a small Louis XVI table. I open it, expecting to find prints of Watteau, of Fragonard. Instead I find naked children got up as fauns or cupids, with the eyes of peasant lads but with a seascape in the background. By Van Gloedel is my first guess, but I draw no inferences. At that moment, glancing down into the courtyard, I see a fawn-coloured limousine of regal proportions roll in, and from it emerge someone who can only be La Badalona. Five minutes later she enters the drawing-room, her progress that of a Spanish galleon breasting the ocean wave. When she notices me she assaults me with cold disdain: "What did you say your name was?"

"I haven't said it, but I will now. Yours most unworthily, Tommaso Mulè."

"Mulè?" she repeats as if these two meagre syllables made her puke. "What do you want? Go away!"

"You ask a question and then countermand it. Either I go and don't answer or I answer and don't go."

One point to me. She gestures me to sit down, holds my eye and waits. I take this moment to give her the once-over: tall as a Grenadier, no make-up, hair cut like a man's, a beak of a nose, an expression of both indolence and arrogance . . . though in compensation a body in all its grandeur still desirable in spite of her fifty years. It floats into my mind that she might be one of the matrons in the *Storia arcana* or the third courtesan in that painting of Carpaccio's . . .

So I put my head down and charge, at the risk of coming a cropper. In any case I've studied my part too well to get tongue-tied at the crucial moment.

"Get ready to turf me out," I begin, but then I blaze away without pausing for breath: "This will take five minutes, so don't interrupt. What I'm going to say is probably slanderous, but don't worry. If it is, please forgive me and let me go, erase me from your memory. If not, believe what I tell you and act accordingly. Without giving me any reply that might compromise you, but simply kicking me out, even literally. That said, here is my trouble. I was the friend of a person lately dead. I am suspected of possessing a certain dubious legacy of his which, if it came to light, would do a lot of harm to a lot of classy people. Rumour has it that you may know something about it. I don't know, I don't think so, in fact I'm certain not. But if by chance there's any truth in the rumour, you should know that I have nothing, that I've got as much to do with it as a cabbage with a cappuccino, I'm as innocent as the day is long. Therefore, to whom it may concern I say I don't want to die for no reason, leave me in peace. That's all I have to say. Now I take my leave."

"You're raving, you should see a doctor," purrs La Badalona. Then she advances to my side, gives me a fiery glare in which I seem to detect a covert hint of admiration, and holds out her hand for me to kiss.

# ELEVEN

# The Filibuster

*Sunday, September 3rd*

We arrive in dribs and drabs for the tenants' meeting. I go upstairs in the company of Pirzio, who for some reason is more expansive than usual. Up in the attic we are met by Adele the cleaning-woman, who has this moment finished putting the room in order. "There were fifty-two of them, now there are fifty-one," she complains. "There's one missing." She is speaking of the chairs kept stacked up in an empty room in the adjacent "Sunflower" building, whence they are fetched three or four times a year for group meetings or the convivial festivities of Christmas and Easter. These are the only occasions on which all of us here in the building, though differing so much from each other, think of ourselves as a family, affiliated by momentary connivance in a party or a show of some kind. It proves that the fact of living in a communal dwelling can act as a mild social adhesive, just such as exists between passengers on a cruise ship or patients taking the waters at Salsomaggiore. In this we are helped by the canonical repetition of rituals: everyone flocking into the meeting-place, cheerful as excursionists; the greetings, more easy-going than in the daily helter-skelter at the doors of the lift; the interest shown by all in discussing the most urgent problems of our communal life; the childlike anticipation of rounding the proceedings off with the entertainments which year after year Crisafulli invents for us, and which are the butt of benevolent mockery, though amid apparently universal applause. A quaint sort of family is ours, priding itself on these superficial cordialities only to rush at each other's throats over some futile point on the agenda with all the violence of football fans.

The shindy doesn't last long as a rule. Leone Mundula lets us get it off our chests for a while and then suddenly snuffs us out with a pitiless diktat, pouring a flood of quibbles and High Court rulings on our intimidated and credulous heads. But today a different wind is blowing. As a result of the threat to raise the rent one can read on all faces a challenge and resolution which, however, Mundula's first honeyed words are sufficient to deflate: "I've booked a telephone call to Los Angeles. In ten minutes. I'll talk to the boss, I'll get something out of him."

With this he goes off and leaves us to talk over the items on the agenda. Seated between Pirzio and Crisafulli, who take no part in the debate, I prefer to look around, among so many necks, seeking the nape of Leah's. She is three rows in front, just visible enough for me to interrogate the few centimetres of her snowy shoulders protruding from a flower-patterned blouse, and the dark bun surmounting a neck of almost depraved slenderness. All minor revelations of that persistent mystery which is herself, despite the day before yesterday's passionate outburst, if it was not a mere boast, about being a guest and participant at La Badalona's party . . . At night, I ask myself? How did our printer friend allow it, father or sugar-daddy as the case may be? Did he know nothing about it? Was it possible?

I am recalled to less ecstatic sights by a certain bustling about at my side on the part of Pirzio. He has extracted from his pocket a piece of card which he hides in his cupped hands, every so often raising his eyes to compare it with the chair in front of him, then with his own, accompanying this with pantomime gestures of his body and face, where sits a look of block-headed satisfaction.

"Woodworm?" I hazard with feigned innocence, but he has already resumed his seat and, as if on purpose to irritate me further, begins to hum the tune of an outdated pop song that makes no sense to speak of:

> Tra-la-la, tra-la-la, tra-la-la,
> Who will it be, who will it be
> To take the lid off? We shall see . . .
> Tra-la-la, tra-la-la, tra-la-la!

After which he assumes such a smug expression that, overcoming my natural pride and reserve, I launch into a string of questions: "Take the lid off what? Is this a quiz? Is there a prize for it?"

To which he replies: "Take your choice, my dear Tommaso, saucepan lids or whited sepulchres."

He laughs his head off and I'd like to sock him one.

This is the first time I've heard him so scandalously communicative, and I am as much amazed as I am riled. Partly because at the same time, on my right, winking his bright little eyes at me, our dramaturge Crisafulli is continually harrying me with the most verbose sales-patter on behalf of this evening's entertainment. Caught between two fires, as if watching a ping-pong match, I encourage each in turn, bestowing my final preference to my left, where Pirzio is still busy with his piece of cardboard and clucking over it with an almost mystical fervour: it must be a little holy picture of Padre Pio. I crane my neck to peep at it out of the corner of my eye, but it's obvious he's no longer worried about my curiosity, indeed indirectly he seems to invite it. Eventually he opens the palm of his hand and flaunts his booty before my eyes: "Identical, eh?"

Identical to what? The photograph shows an object of a mass-produced kind: a chair with its legs in the air at the foot of what looks like the pier of a bridge. A chair however – and herein lies the significance of his question – of the same shape, wood and colour as those on which we are resting our behinds . . .

What does this mean? In virtue of what spirit of initiative has this "Sunflower" chair migrated so far from its native roof-beam as to find itself in effigy in the hands of a policeman? I say policeman because a few minutes ago a cast-iron conviction entered my head: that Pirzio is a kind of Serpico, who has infiltrated our community in the guise of a tenant in order to get a close look, I don't say at the mystery of Tir's death, since he was already here when that happened, but at some evil deed of earlier date. I think back to the gang of young drug addicts, to the thousands of words I've caught Mundula mumbling into the telephone, to the dubious activities of Lo Surdo. Ah, there is no shortage of food for investigation in Flower City, as in any assemblage of human beings, or any human heart.

Well then, if this is the way things are, if Pirzio really is a police officer, what is the significance of his interest in the fact that the chair in the photo is the same as the real chairs lined up before our eyes? Could it be . . . but while a hypothesis flashes to mind it is promptly doused by the re-entry of Mundula and his accession to the throne, viz., to the armchair shortly to form one of the props in Crisafulli's one-act play. From this he now rises and begins as follows:

"Shortly before he died my father asked to have a stick with an iron ferrule buried with him. 'To walk with if need be,' he said, 'and if need be to strike with.' I presume he alluded to a showdown with God, the only being he deigned to have as an enemy. He was that hard to please! From him I learnt to be a man of few words and to decide, when necessary, by the power of the sceptre. This is by way of telling you that our village, if I may so call it, is going through a bad patch and requires agreement, authority . . . "

Discontented murmurs in the room. A voice from the back: "Anything new about the rent?"

Mundula smiles, though it is more of a grimace than a smile: "I talked the boss round. No rise in the rents for a year. Only eviction for non-payers."

The applause is general, except for Bisceglie of course.

Mundula resumes in a despotic manner that gets my goat: "So today you can bicker as much as you like, but not for more than ten minutes per item. After which, take a vote and there's an end of it. If there's no clear decision, I will decide, *quia nominor leo* . . ." And here, fatuously, he imitated the MGM lion, giving rise to obsequious laughter. "Before you," he continued, "you have the sheet with the agenda. Give it a quick read, then whoever wants to can start the ball rolling."

"My God," I thought, "are we here to take the Tennis Court Oath?" And before anyone had so much as opened his mouth I had let my mind go wandering among its vapours; so that the concert of voices that followed, entwining high and low, loud and soft, a seething of rages, agreements, passions, came to my ears as intermittently as wind through the slats of shutters.

I had fixed my gaze, as before, on Leah's shoulders, and in carnal thoughts of the woman I spent the hour or more the debate lasted, grasping only snatches of it and confining myself to raising my hand, almost always at random, whenever a vote was called for. It was like those times when, after a bathe, we stretch out on the sand with our hearing still dulled with sea-water, and lulled by the distant sound of the undertow we fall half asleep. It was not that I failed to follow the ideas and opinions, but that I felt myself to be light years away. I would therefore be unable to report on the session, were it not that I have the minutes before me. Which for future reference, as is my duty as chronicler, with a few embellishments I here summarize.

The first item on the agenda, which regards the freedom to keep animals in the building, causes an immediate clash between animal lovers and others. In favour is Donna Marzia, and even more so Mariposa, the owner of a Pekinese; uncertain is the stance of the Garaffas, in controversy with mice but favourable to cats; charmingly eccentric is Placido, who cannot bear cats but has a soft spot for mice: "On the TV lately I saw an experiment in which they measured the intelligence of mice. The creatures are shut into a maze at the end of which is some food. A count is then made of the minutes each mouse takes to learn the route and repeat it when called upon to do so in less time than before. Well then . . . "

"These mice are pure imagination," broke in Buozzi. "No one sees them except Signora Garaffa."

To which Placido placidly replied: "Not necessarily. I think they might well inhabit this building as extremely crafty stowaways. Nor would I bet on our winning this struggle between mice and men . . . "

Mundula's intervention at this point shuts everybody up: "This is slandering the whole condominium. Buozzi is right, the mice are menopausal fantasies. And I want no animals in this building, except bipeds with their rent paid up."

For their different reasons Bisciglie and Signora Garaffa look down at the ground, and the matter is closed.

Troubles with the lift, in their turn, provoke both mutterings and outcries. What with breakdowns and maintenance it costs too much. Should we abolish it and use the stairs, with consequent benefit to our health, as suggested by Buozzi, who in any case lives on the first floor? Install a slot-machine? Charge more from people living on the upper floors, who make more use of it? Opinions differ, while there is universal scorn for those thoughtless enough to leave the door open (Placido at my side: "Everyone has their hackles up, but what's the betting they're among the guilty parties?").

Worse still – it is Signora Lo Surdo who, with some embarrassment, brings the matter up – if one is forced to go up on foot to get the lift going again, and finds it jammed on purpose, with someone inside it clumsily adjusting their dress . . .

A voice in the audience, though impossible to tell whose, hisses the names of the twins and Maurizio, occasioning loud lamentations, both paternal and maternal, of which the minutes give only a discreet indication, followed by an "etcetera" laden with meaning.

Concerning the disturbance caused by jazz records we have a long, impassioned defence by Johnnie, contradicted by all and sundry with the sole, timid exception of myself during an interval in my reverie. More peacefully resolved is the dispute about the eviction which threatens our trumpeter. Donna Marzia offers to pay his back rent: she has sold a Piranesi *Carcere d'invenzione* for a good price and flatters herself on her philanthropy. Finally comes the case of Mariposa. At this point, to be honest, I woke somewhat from my torpor. The paradox is that all the tenants from first to last have a soft spot for this male lady, but they don't want to go further than that. On account of her questionable acquaintances, her coming home at dawn, her outrageous dress, the risk of infection, and the whole aura of sin that surrounds her person which, they say, might pollute the good name of the establishment. As a lover of lost causes I am about to get to my feet, but Mundula silences me and settles the matter in a few words: "I am not a puritan," he says, "but in these things one must cut the Gordian knot. You, Mariposa, may do as you please, but elsewhere. Here you must dress decently, we wish for no more fancy-dress parties in the building."

Mariposa weeps, my lone vote does her no good. She has to give in or leave.

The last items, listed under the heading "Various", are swiftly dealt with though to me they seem the most pressing problems: the numerous desertions, decampings, terminations of lease; the others already announced; the visit of the engineering experts following the alarm about cracks until then ignored or ridiculed. Garaffa makes a feeble attempt to speak on the subject, but gets bogged down in terms like phreatic strata and landslips that cause annoyance all round. Mundula interrupts him and the poor man utters not another word. "If," declares the lawyer mercilessly, "one were not forced to show indulgence to an obvious incompetent, I would now mortify him with the reassuring assessment of the municipal experts. You must take my word for it that all is well." And in a trice he is getting everyone's signature and announcing Crisafulli's performance. Two minutes are enough to prepare the set: the chairman's seat in the middle, facing us; to the right a bench with a stool before it, and on it a ream of white paper; to the left a courtroom-type bar. Above the whole a banner bearing the legend: "Montecitorio".

It is the moment Crisafulli has been awaiting for the best part of a year. He makes his way confidently forward between the rows of seats. He looks unusually tall, and is in fact wearing shoes with excessively high heels. "Don't tell me it's a buskin job," chuckles Placido, intent on not missing a single detail of the pantomime. But Crisafulli, turning to face us: "Signor Leone Mundula, Signorina Leah Buozzi, I need your assistance. Two tiny parts, I have the words here," and he flourishes two scraps of paper. The chosen pair willingly join him "on stage", but behind his back they nudge each other in the ribs. Finally he tells them where to sit:

Mundula resumes his throne and Leah takes the stenographer's stool. Then the actor, fixing his gaze on us: "Ladies and gentlemen," he starts, "here I stand before you. The work I am about to perform is entitled *The Filibuster*, and you have all the rights of both audience and chorus. A chorus of Members in a House of Parliament, with full liberty, of course, to interrupt, boo or applaud. As for me, I perform seven roles, those of designer, director, publicist, prompter, chucker-out, electrician and protagonist. Not to mention, you understand, the sole author of the *opus* on which I shall shortly raise the curtain."

Plainly he has taken the thing far more seriously than in the past. Both in his speech and in his very person there was a sort of desperate clowning that, in me at any rate, induced respect. There was in his voice a note of hysteria that suggested he was on the verge of derangement and affliction.

"Time and place," he announced didactically; then paused, and continued with great solemnity: "Imagine a time in the future, far in the future, after the discovery of the elixir that prolongs life for ever. A World Assembly is held . . . "

Here he broke off, pointed to the banner reading "Montecitorio" and said hastily: "Take no notice, it's a mistake. In the first draft the action was to have been confined to Italy. Simply read UNO and on we go."

To a burst of encouraging applause on our part he replied with a bow and continued: "A World Assembly, therefore, in which are debated the problems surrounding our newly-acquired immortality. The Chairman of this assembly – and well he deserves the honour – is our well-beloved administrator, who for lack of extras also represents the government as a whole. Leah is the stenographer, while I am the interpolating delegate."

Leone and Leah were swift to back him up: "I am the President of the World Government," proclaimed Mundula as he went to occupy the Chair in the centre of the stage. "I am the lovely secretary," chirruped Leah with affected vivacity, and mincingly seated herself on the right.

"Thank you, thank you," laughed Crisafulli like a child, then he in turn took his place on the imaginary stage and, turning his back to us, went on:

"I must say a few words of introduction. For lack of time and costumes, I have not been able to dress appropriately. Your imaginations will enable you to see me clad in a blue coat like a hospital doctor's. On my head is a straw hat pierced here and there by candles, such as Van Gogh wore when he went out painting at night. In short, from numerous details you are led to suspect that I am off my head. And now, here's yours . . . "

So saying he hands Mundula his part and motions him into action. "The order of the day," reads Mundula in sonorous tones, "concerns the turning into law of Government Decree no. etc., bearing extension no. etc., at article etc., which reads as follows:

"ARTICLE ONE: Having effect at once and immediately, within the territory of the Earthly Republic and regarding the citizens of the same it is prohibited to die at any time or place, by whatever means and whatever the weather. To this end it is imperiously laid down that each and every citizen be vaccinated every six months with a phial of 'Athanos', of recent and happy discovery, in addition to the daily postprandial ingestion of a teaspoonful of 'Telebios' as produced by the State laboratories. Defaulters, whether motivated by a stubborn suicidal project or by intrinsic thoughtlessness or juvenile negligence, or due to the influence of pessimistic philosophies, whenever caught in the flagrant act of death and in possession of a corpse still warm, shall be liable to numerous lashes of the cat-o'-nine-tails, to be executed upon the aforesaid corpse. Should the latter, owing to burns or other abrasive or deleterious mishap, be lacking or otherwise unusable, it shall be substituted by a life-size dummy of the criminal, this penalty to be broadcast live on Euroglobovision TV.

"ARTICLE TWO: Abolished concurrently, the Treasury being charged with the expropriation of their property movable and otherwise, are the following institutions and commercial concerns pertaining to the former deprecated and heinous practice of dying: the Order of Doctors, Pharmacists and Undertakers, the Loved-One Fan Clubs, the Friends of Sylvia Plath, as well as many here omitted for the sake of brevity but to be found in Appendix No. 1.

"ARTICLE THREE: The Military Authority is hereby ordered to administer solid and liquid foods to the hunger-strikers now encamped at the crossroads of the Quattro Fontane here in Rome and to throw the instigator into irons as soon as his speechifying renders him identifiable.

"On the above proposed decree debate is now open. The Rt Hon. Crusafulli has asked to speak. He has the floor."

"Oof!" concluded Mundula, impromptu.

Crisafulli moved slowly to take his stand beside Mundula, offering us a view of his left profile which, as he was wont to say, was scarcely that of a Greek statue. His tone of voice was neutral to start with, rather professorial, but little by little became more animated:

"Numerous and greatly vilified," he began, "are the techniques of filibustering from the benches of the most diverse parliaments and assemblies, and to such an extent are they plainly injurious no less to the industrious larynxes of those who hold forth as to the passive ears of the listeners, and in short, to speak plainly and so as not to overstrain the frail mental powers of Mr President, opinion both public and private is so fed up with our hoary old non-stop filibusters that . . . "

There was insurrection throughout the audience: "What d'you

think you're doing? Who d'you think you are? What language is this, Double Dutch?"

Crisafulli crowed with delight: "Ha! I see you've entered the spirit of the thing. Very good, very good!" Then, as pompous as before: "In a word, we can no longer tolerate the traditional forms of filibustering. So that when a speaker, such as myself at this moment, boldly dares to try out a new one, he should not be greeted with jeers and protests, but rather with indulgent expectation and curiosity even on the part of the members of the hostile government, in this case absent, with the sole exception of that sleepyhead up there . . . "

And so saying he flashed a torch, till then concealed, on the face of Mundula, catching him with his eyes almost shut, if not entirely so. The pause acted like an invitation to the spectators, intimidated until now both by the incomprehensible bombast of the discourse and by their long-standing affection for the orator. A variety of sounds therefore arose, together with a few subdued catcalls. Which did not prevent Crisafulli from continuing: "Curiosity, I was saying, not only on the part of the accomplices of power, but on that of anyone here present, whether usher or apprentice reporter or parliamentary commentator or spectator in the gallery or blond stenographer . . . "

Leah, who was raven-haired, looked up in surprise. But Crisafulli: "Blond, *dixi*, and that should be enough to exclude you, darksome as you are, so don't be angry, I'm not getting at you. Just see to setting down my words with professional fingers, thus rendering them less perishable. For if later . . . "

The booing now ceased to be occasional and swelled into a single continuous roar. But he went on: "Colleagues and fellow Members, be patient and do not waste your substance, you will tire yourselves out. It is my intention to speak until either I die or you do. With this very act violating the disastrous law you intend to impose on the community of nations, and demonstrating that it is iniquitous and inapplicable. Nor by this do I intend to say that living, and even living for ever, is not a commendable thing for those who have a taste for it. But those who haven't ought not to be coerced by your decrees. Which should therefore be revoked. Or at least emended. In the sense that death should be declared legal for those who make a written request for it, duly signed. And I add, for your solace, that such request must be accompanied by documents which justify its submission, and that a Council of Wisemen must be convened to decide on its acceptance or rejection. This is my earnest wish, or indeed ours, since behind me there are thousands who, fed up with or disdainful of or nauseated by the general euphoria, urge me to speak expressly on their behalf. Allow me and allow us, therefore, to die, if such be our wish. For if you are against us, I swear that I shall stand here and from floor to ceiling of this House block every one of your attempts at legislation, and moreover . . . "

The insurrection was total. Most were laughing, to tell the truth, but none the less continued to boo, hiss and hammer their heels on the floor. A brutish booing showed that some key had come into play. But the man would not desist: "Ladies and gentlemen, bear with me. I will improve as I go on. I prefer the poison in the head rather than the tail. You must blame the style of this exordium of mine on naught but a whim and a fancy. I well know that the eulogy of death that I am about to improvise, rather than flashy preciosities and linguistic galli-maufries, calls for the colours and palls of night, and modest, muted tones, like any other mournful thing. Nor at the outset would I have dared to sound the salpinx and the trumpet, if at my side, as formerly, I had the venerable white locks of Senator Eugenic Montale. Of whom I will now read you . . . "

He could not continue. Everyone was on his feet, even

Mundula was booing, there was no stopping the uproar.

"I will explain!" yelled the poet, but no one paid any attention. "I will explain all! Now comes the best part, now comes my apologia for dying a good death."

When he realized it was all over, Crisafulli mounted a chair and for a moment asserted himself over the small mob that had invaded the imaginary stage, still laughing and booing together as in an endless student rag. We saw him swiftly draw a revolver, point it at his temple. In the instant silence that came over us, no one had the courage or the presence of mind to stop him pulling the trigger. But all we heard was a ludicrous click, a sort of schoolboy fart, followed on the part of all present by an enormous guffaw of relief.

"I didn't know," he said, more to himself than to us. "I didn't know it wasn't loaded . . . "

Hard to believe him, of course, knowing how in Chekhov's characters, from Uncle Vanya to Platonov, he cherished the delight they took in gestures that failed to come off . . .

# TWELVE

# Firstfruits of Revelation

*Monday, September 4th*

Thus it was that Girolamo Crisafulli's insanity began; or rather, it was now that we saw it openly erupt, whereas its development had been below the surface. Everyone was shocked, though something that should have alerted us, or at least struck us as a curious impediment of sense, was his nervous tic of suddenly breaking off while conversing in the most amiable manner, and bending down to search the ground for a button he claimed had fallen off. And this without ever being able to show that there was any trace of one missing from any of his garments, inner or outer. We put this down to a bizarre personality given to the make-believe of the theatre. Now that his malady had exploded in such an obvious form, we were not too surprised the next day by the arrival of an ambulance and two men in white coats, or by the scene with him at the barred window declaiming the opening of a *Jeronimus pro morte sua*, presumably a postscript to the interrupted *Filibuster*. There was only a handful of us on the pavement to see him off, but I at any rate, as I went back indoors, felt the need to reassure myself about my mental health. How many impulses, equal but opposite: a sedentary hypochondriac and at the same time an extroverted, peripatetic investigator; disillusioned with everything yet head over heels in love; an inkstained compulsive scribbler but averse

to that confidentiality with an unknown reader which writing
demands. Ah yes, unknown reader, it is high time I owned up
to a prejudice against you. If I have said nothing until now it
has been deliberate: I was anxious to keep you at arm's length
but at the same time not to put you off any more than my pages
do by themselves. Now that the end is in sight I owe you a
declaration of some sort, if not of disdain at least of distrust.
The same distrust that prevents me from talking to strangers on
a train, that makes me get up and move whenever someone
sits down to read his newspaper on the same park-bench as
me . . . It has always been this way, ever since the day when, in
a lay-by along the road to Damascus, struck by the thunderbolt
of profanity, I abjured the god of literature. Since then I have
written only by way of intimate soliloquy or medicament or
good cheer (or else for money, of course, and in that case, alas,
accepting and desiring you). A conversion in reverse, after so
much faithful fanaticism. Accompanied by no more than mild
remorse. An apostate of small vices and small virtues, I will
not be one to suffer the punishment of that priest I once read
about in some Fleur du Mal or other, who was reduced to
insanity by the sheer pride of his rebellion. Thank you very
much, *après moi pas de déluge*, at the most a meagre drizzle.

Now that I've got that off my chest let's start again. As long as
you don't take me too seriously when I let my tongue wag as I
did just now; nor, in my self-denunciations, should you rule
out a dash of mischief. After that, *respice finem*, we'll see at the
end. To arrive at which I am conceited enough to believe that
all I require is a lucid mind and a pen that doesn't gush. I have
already made a note (you remember?) of the sore afflictions
I've come up against in the course of the adventure that I now
live through and write about, that I have pompously labelled

Pathos, Eros and Phobos. I am now convinced that a more scrupulous philology is required to make sense of so many contradictions, with or without capital letters. Naturally I would like each piece to fall into place as in the supreme thrillers of the 1930s; but the questions I am chewing over are for the moment getting no digestible answers, but only tissue-paper reasons and hypotheses. So I tell myself that the first thing is to take a census of the problems, list them in order of import-ance, and devote myself with loving fervour to each in turn, like an impartial polygamist with his women. I have counted my thorny enigmas and they are seven. I shall give myself a week to work them out, starting by putting each as a heading to a blank page in my diary. At the top of the first is a name, the name of Leah.

Leah is the key to everything. An eye-witness by her own admission in a moment of folly, she alone can sort out the tangle of the licentious binge. Besides – and for me a far more salutary operation – she alone with a decisive yes or no can tame the systoles of my quaking heart. To her, therefore, I devote my preliminary research.

Wishing to speak to her in secret, I mount guard at my usual skylight waiting for Buozzi's pointed shoes to pass before me, as happens at seven-fifty every morning on their way to catch the eight o'clock at the bus-stop near the fountain on the other side of Flower City, by the firmly bolted entrance to the unfinished "Sunflower". I don't have to wait a moment longer: his feet are punctual to the split second. As soon as I spot them I abandon my guardhouse and rush outside. I want to make sure he really does leave. I therefore shadow him for the whole of the two hundred metres between him and the bus-shelter. A stack of newspapers makes an adequate hiding-place. I even buy one, a copy of the dear old "Spyglass", not only as an additional mask for my face but for reasons of legitimate vanity, inasmuch as it contains my first effort as a special correspondent. A pity I had to sign it with a pseudonym, Zadig, which few will understand. And an even greater pity that it contains five parts guesswork, four parts fabrication and only one, and a small part at that, of facts or what are presumed to be such. I could do no less if I was to content Bendidio and justify my advance.

Anyway, here is the bus. Buozzi gets on, away he goes. All that now separates me from Leah are a few hundred paces, a closed door, the armour of her silence. Working in my favour are surprise, my glib tongue and the intensity of desire. We'll see.

On the way back I again pass the wooden paling that surrounds the abandoned building-site in which stands the "Sunflower". Unfinished and boarded up as it is, it remains impressive in its way. The project of the whole complex, with its mighty stone towers linked by a system of flying bridges, was not too bad. As it stands now, this crude pile of stones perfectly well deserves Bisceglie's contemptuous sobriquet of Shit Building, or the more erudite one of Cacciola's Folly with which the philosopher Placido, a Conrad fan, one day dubbed it. As you raise your eyes you see dozens of storeys heaped one upon the other, half of them boarded up, the remainder open to wind and weather, the eyes of their windows now blinded, now staring out of the dirty yellow of the corroded, peeling, skeletal masonry.

While I've still got my nose in the air I stumble over a bump in the ground, and I can't help thinking of something in Tir's story. In fact all the indications he mentioned are right here before me: the uneven ground, the piazza, the fountain . . . Yet he spoke of having travelled by car for an hour, while from the "Carnation" to the "Sunflower" takes barely ten minutes even on foot. Unless of course . . .

*          *

I already knew that she wouldn't open the door, so I had a note ready in my pocket to slip under it. It said: "Leah, you need me. If you are guilty I will be your accomplice, if you are innocent I will be your lawyer. In either case I know tricks galore for both of us. I too, indirectly, am in jeopardy. By saving you I will save myself.

"P.S. (important): I love you."

It works. The door is not flung wide, but it opens a crack, and through the crack her wary but interested face peers out at me. And I peer back at this woman I claim to love.

Pale, above everything else. Her whiteness was what struck me about her the very first time. Now it seems to have increased beyond all belief: worthy of a TV commercial. Even then (I can't remember if I told you) it reminded me of an image in a poet I love: "dark as a lily". True of her as of no one else, such is the sense of puzzling enigma that charges her whiteness with the most ambiguous powers and elects her at one and the same time the emblem of frosty aloofness and the last word in dazzlement. White is the colour of the clouds, of paradise, of the face of God; white are the shrouds of ghosts, the unspeakable horror of nothingness, the last thing seen by the eyes of Gordon Pym . . .

Nor would I ever have thought I could have fallen in love with her, I who of women, as of skies, of food, of words, have always demanded some sulphurous taste or odour, an over-emphasis, an excess, a sting of garlic, a bacillus . . . And yet, here I am immersed in the half-witted worship of this powdered Columbine, this dolly of the snows . . . I whose eyes and ears were tutored by the howl of the Mediterranean in sun-parched piazzas.

Whereas she . . . Arctic! Sidereal! "Miss Frigidaire" is the irreverent nickname bestowed on her in this building (which pullulates with nicknames, my own being "Mattia Pascal", after Pirandello's famous character). I correct hers sentimentally to "Miss Moonlight", while dwelling on how much fire must smoulder beneath the frost of her flesh. And how this, naked between the sheets, might melt at my side, kindle, burst into flame . . . I think of the burrow of her sex where surely flows the abundance of her blood as into a swollen heart. I think of the mellow saxophone of her voice, that in each modulation or pause emulates the artifices of a long-drawn-out orgasm.

"Leah," I begin, taking her hand and running out of words. She withdraws her hand, closes the door behind us and motions me to sit facing her, with between us a low table littered with old bonbonnières and cheap knick-knacks.

"Well," says she, "have you brought the film?"

"I haven't got it, but I have an idea. First you tell me about that night. You've admitted you were there."

She thinks about that for rather too long. I am tempted to bully her, but restrain myself. At last it all comes out in a rush:

"That night's not important, what matters are the nights before. You know I live with my stepfather and that I don't lead the life of a nun. He was the first, after my mother died, and I consented. I was little more than a child, he told me it would cure my acne. To tell the truth, he was right about that. In his way he was a passionate torturer, and for a long time I let him have his way. Finally I came to my senses, and could put up with him less and less. A thousand times I thought of leaving, but where could I go and what could I do? Work as a maid? A prostitute? In any case I would need money to get me on my feet.

"At this point, enter Mundula. He pays a visit on some pretext and gets interested in me. I was lying, there in your room, when I put on a show of indignation. I did it to regain the confidence of Buozzi, who was having doubts. The fact is I've used Mundula for money, with only a little petting in return for it. He's a listless libertine and was happy with that. But he paid me, and how! It was a sort of Round Robin: Buozzi gave me the rent money, I passed it on to you, you handed it over to Mundula. Then he gave it back to me and I hid the money in my mattress. Until, taking advantage of the fact that Buozzi had been taken on by a newspaper for night work, he offered me some saucier business. All I had to do was strip off at a small private party, nothing more than that. The money was good, and I also liked the prospect of doing something devilish. I said yes."

As I listened I went from surprise to surprise. I was intrigued by this Leone Mundula, patron of and participant in orgies. I tried to picture him in acts of debauchery. Nothing doing: for me he always retained a derisory cache-sexe, and the short cream-coloured socks that were such an eyesore whenever he crossed his legs.

On Leah's part came another long silence, counterpointed this time by an unexpected display of emotion in the form of short sobs deep in the throat followed by quiet, copious and almost interminable weeping. What to do? The girl seemed to have virtually unlimited reserves . . . I get up, circle the table, sit down beside her, then lift her onto my knee, affectionately and purely compassionately, without the least tremor of lust. A long-buried paternal instinct surfaces in the gestures with which I smooth her hair, wipe away her tears. She calms down at last, taking up her tale again with such haste and eagerness as to suggest that confessing is for her a physical pleasure, a relieving detumescence. Something much like it happens to me, and I am taken back to the time when, during a fit of colic, I felt the sudden relief of the gall-stone emerging from my urethra. But she was once more pouring forth words and tears:

"So late in the evening I set off with Mundula, the appointment was close by, in a place I'd never have dreamt of, on the first floor of the 'Sunflower'. The guests got there through a side door which every member of the club has a key to, but Mundula and I took an inner, secret route, right up to the lofts and down again without any risk of being seen. We made our way along dark passages and bridges between the finished building and the abandoned one with only a torch to show us where to put our feet on leftover bits of scaffolding and roughcast concrete. The air was cool but smelt musty, in spite of the yawning great windows without any glass in them. A rat slunk between our feet – if one can use such a word of a rat – and vanished into the dark. And finally we reached our destination, which was all lit up and already crowded with people . . . "

I broke in: "What about Tir? Was he there too? And Dorotea, and Ersilia? What about La Badalona?"

"Tir was there, but quite unaware of me, of Mundula and everything else, even of where he was. They'd carted him all over town just to muddle him, and now he was sitting on the only chair in the room and letting off flashbulbs one after the other, when and where he was told to. We posed in front of him wearing something less than a figleaf and entwined together in the maddest and most grotesque postures. I went along with it, a little scared but determined to make the most money for the least effort.

"They were all laughing, drinking, singing. I wasn't at all surprised to recognize our late co-tenants the drug-shooting students, who had always seemed to me not merely tolerated but in some obscure way protected by Mundula. Evidently, like the others, they were old hands at the business. I was a beginner, and not the only one. There were two other girls who I learnt had run away from home in the country and had been bribed at the station by that hulking fellow standing by the door, a sort of brainless Hercules with the arms of a butcher. I asked Mundula who he was. 'Blasco, La Badalona's lover,' he whispered, and pointed out the lady in question: a gigantic woman with the most incredible breasts that hung down to her belly. Completely unrestrained yet somehow majestic in her ageing nakedness, like one of those queens you see in films about black Africa, Taitus or whatever they're called.

"So now you must imagine the scene: blades of light piercing the night and us, after parading in front of the camera, sitting in a circle on the ground, smoking pipes of opium and gazing awe-struck out of the windows at the starry sky. Looking at the sky has always made me feel that way . . . "

"So all that went on down there was nudism and opium-smoking?"

"Not all, no. That was just for starters. Then came the main dish which began with everyone giving themselves a fix. I didn't want to do it, and as it was my first time they didn't force me to. The two girls did, though, and you know how it ended up."

"What happened then?"

"Well then, as the only one in my right mind, although a little dazed from the opium, I watched the excesses that followed with a mixture of ecstasy and nausea: the furious and sterile fellatios, the sexual acrobatics, the bodies rolling on the floor in a mess of crap, sperm and vomit, until the last flicker of sensual enthusiasm faded and they lay there like corpses after a massacre in a public square. It was hours before they realized that one of them was a real corpse."

"And you, during all those hours, just looked on and nothing else?"

"Nothing else. And not from qualms of conscience or virtuous modesty either. The opium had left me in a state of rapture and clairvoyance. The scenes unfolding before my eyes were like pictures on a tapestry or in stained glass, and I only had to close my eyes and my lids became a palette where I mixed colours of incredible splendour. I saw ever-widening circles of sparks giddily spiralling up towards a stationary sun. A sun that was the pupil of my own eye which, way out there beyond me, had become the radiant vanishing point of the universe. When I shook myself out of it night was already giving way to dawn, and through the window I saw the air slowly change from deep blue to dullish purple. I fled."

Everything as clear as daylight? Well, nearly. There remained the mystery of the unfindable film, and other lesser mysteries. But what made my confusion worse confounded was the overall unreality of the thing, the same feeling you have at the theatre, one of temporary identification with the action on stage behind which, though dulled perhaps, awareness of everyday reality does not cease its vigilance. Besides that, what Leah had not so much told me as sung to me was scarcely more than an opera libretto, a melodious scenario, maybe even a vaudeville turn.

In short, however hard the girl tried to persuade me it was true, I found it hard to visualize the event as fact rather than fiction. In point of logic, if you like, the links held together, but not all of them, and some less than others. I swiftly censured the weaker ones, being too wrapped up in trying to understand the complex nature of my emotions. This woman whose breath and odour were even now mingling with mine . . . I felt the urge to reject her and at the same time to possess her. And to possess her not as a purely sexual liberation but as a confirmation of the truth, a way of setting the seal of real life on what might be simply a trick of the eyesight. For the fact is that the more closely I embraced this woman, and felt her adhere to my skin, the more she seemed to be speaking from some nebulous distance. I finally risked a clumsy kiss on her hair; then her neck, her lips. She did not reciprocate, but inertly she yielded herself. This yielding of hers, or so it seemed to me, was a deep-rooted habit and condescension of the limbs, which at this moment no longer obeyed any mental restraint. So I had her on the shoddy carpet there in the living-room, with a final grunt from each of us, and thereafter between us neither a word nor a tear.

"I'm pushing fifty and you'd better know it." That is what I would have liked to tell her, but I keep mum. Lying side by side, bearing the entire weight of her shoulder on the arm wound around her, I can't bring myself to wriggle free for fear of waking her. Her closed eyes are that good at feigning sleep. Eventually a fierce spasm of cramp gets the better of me, and I give her a shake. She opens her eyes, now perfectly clear, belligerent:

"I love to be loved," she proclaims. "I don't love loving. In any case, all I have in my heart at the moment is fear. And not one fear, but two: that the photos of me come to light and Buozzi sees them; that the drug gang remember I was there and consider me a danger. Remember what happened to Tir."

Plunged back into the urgency of the old, familiar, maddening reality, I get to my feet, adjust my clothes and become grave and rational: "You're not counting a third enemy," I say. "The police. So far they're lying doggo, but they've certainly got their hands on something. Dorotea, for instance . . . "

"Oh, her!" she exclaims. "She's a born goose, she went on a trip the first minute. I don't suppose she could remember or denounce a single thing. Just think that to get rid of her, while some people were dealing with Ersilia's body, others tied her to a chair, all floppy as she was, to make it easier to carry her. Then they hoisted her into a van and dumped her on the Embankment somewhere."

The chair, the missing chair, the fifty-second . . . The only chair in the room, on which Tir had been sitting, borrowed no doubt from Adele's storeroom only to reappear abandoned in a deserted spot in the city, as well as in a black-and-white photo in Pirzio's pocket! Pirzio therefore had a hand in this; he was a cop on the lookout for clues and proofs. I was sure of it before, but now it was confirmed. The man must be watched.

Leah passed a hand across my eyes as if to wipe away a tumult of thoughts and bring me back to the present: "I don't love you," she repeated. "I don't love anyone. Not so far, at least."

I heard these words with a relief that astonished me. Heavens alive, what sort of man was I, would I ever understand the first thing about myself? The truth is that brief entry into her body had drained and purged me of any coagulation of love. Like unblocking a sink. It was therefore simply politeness that made me ask her: "So far, eh? And tomorrow?"

"There won't be any tomorrows. I've decided to run away and I don't want company. I'm only waiting for the case to be closed so that my escape won't make them suspect me."

"But," I objected, "what about your yielding yourself just now?"

"Purely technical," she replied, and indeed she seemed quite a different person from the one who had just wept such a flood of bitter salt tears. "A down payment on the photos you said you'll give me. You told me you had an idea, didn't you?"

"An idea yes, but give me time . . . "

She didn't insist, but quickly took my hands between the two of hers, and grasped them hard: two lukewarm pigeons in a grip of ice. I felt as if I were the woman and she the man.

"Tell me about yourself," she said, sweetening at last. "As I said, so far you're nothing to me. Try and give me an idea of what you're really like."

"My name is Tommaso Mulè," I droned wearily. "I am forty-nine years old. Married and separated. A journalist and writer by ambition, at present unemployed but taken on for the time being as voluntary Trappist and general factotum in a block of flats. In my youth available for the most diverse occupations: movie extra in Biblical and Roman epics, claqueur at the Opera House, sandwich-man for cosmetics and theatrical productions. When you were a little girl you might have seen me up and down Via Barberini with my two placards, one in front and one behind . . . And it always fell to my lot to advertise the most ridiculous first nights: *The Magnificent Cuckold*, *The Man Who Gets Slapped* . . . "

"You know I never leave the house," she said, and immediately stiffened. Someone had knocked. We leapt to our feet, she motioned me towards the kitchen cupboard and shut me in. Meanwhile, "Who is it?" she asked in a sleepy, time-gaining sort of voice.

"Leone," replied the tones of Mundula. She opened the door and I sharpened my ears.

"Just a word or two," said the administrator, "to tell you not to worry. I know a few people at the police station and I know they're floundering in the dark. The film is nowhere to be found, Dorotea, more imbecile than ever, has gone back to her village, Ersilia's death has been classified as accidental, due to drug abuse with the complicity of persons unknown. So keep cool and wait for things to calm down. I've brought you some money."

There followed a long silence. Shut in where I was, I had no idea what was going on. I even suspected that with the Esperanto of sign-language Leah might reveal my presence and put our visitor on the red alert. I was wrong. At next hearing Mundula's voice was placid enough, it betrayed no anxiety whatever: "The parties are suspended for a while, for obvious reasons. And not only to be on the safe side. La Badalona is, so to speak, in mourning. Her daughter – you don't know her, she wasn't there that time – has run away . . . "

"Run away?"

"Yes, and just imagine: with her mother's jewellery and her kept man . . . "

"Who? The man on the motorbike?"

"No other, with Blasco, the irresponsible fart responsible for all our troubles."

Very good, this piece of the jigsaw had also slotted into place. For a moment I was tempted to make a sudden appearance and lay all my cards on the table and create a sensation. But it then occurred to me that, locked in from outside like the lovers in the cupboards beloved of Feydeau, I would have had to go through the farce of knocking to be let out.

I therefore stayed in my excruciating broom-closet and patiently waited for Mundula to take his leave. I didn't have long to wait.

His last words as I heard them were: "Even the rich weep." After which came the sound of the front-door closing.

He was certainly referring to La Badalona, but I would never have suspected him of such a weakness for soap opera.

# THIRTEEN

# Hunt-the-thimble

*Monday, September 4th*

Farewell Leah. A silent farewell I bid her as I leave her room. I have always been amazed at the speed with which I repudiate my most fervent passions. Only that on all other occasions there has always been some trifling thing at the root of my satiety: an off-putting odour, a coarse tone of voice, an ill-expressed thought. But not this time: Leah is glacial and impetuous, candid and immoral enough to appeal to me. I really don't know what excuses to find for this sudden divorce other than the disenchantment which unfailingly follows on the possession of a woman, and (especially) the indolence of a heart weary of beating. As if love were indeed a tachycardiac crisis – racing pulse, gasping breath, the feeling that one's end is near – after which, having swallowed and absorbed a propaphenon tablet, everything becomes subservient to the healthy rhythms of nature. The same happens to me, though I cannot understand the chemistry that has helped to cure me.

That said, my promise to help the woman still holds good. To find and destroy the dangerous photographs appears to me the seriocomical mission of my mature years. For if I brought it off without letting anyone know, I would at one and the same time make fools of Bendidio, the police, and all the stuffed shirts in the city. I would be leaving Tir unavenged – that is true. But, thinking it over, am I really all that sure his death wasn't an accident after all? Since I learnt that the demoniac motorcyclist had with no ulterior motive preferred the daughter to the mother, the charge of being a heartless killer has lost a little force; nor does it seem so necessary to link the deaths of Tir and Ersilia. Nor do I quite see what interest Badalona & Co. had in bumping off the repository of the missing treasure . . .

Enough of that. I now happen to pass Mariposa in the company of a gentleman who fails to recognize me, and whom I pretend not to recognize. She scatters happiness through both her eyes, and her nibbled lips are open in a laugh without motive.

She introduces us: "Radaelli, do you know Mulè?" I give a curt bow and make an excuse to be on my way, thinking to myself that the lost sheep has come back to the fold. Unless of course it's a wolf . . . In any case it's up to them, they don't scandalize me, I actually like them. I only hope that she gets away with being dressed as a woman despite the dire sentence of the Assembly . . .

A moment later I hear a clickety-clack rushing up behind me. It is Mariposa who has broken loose from her Skyriot Achilles and is now hot on my heels. "Newsrag!" she calls to me. "Here, Newsrag!" I stop and listen. "I wanted to tell you two things. One is really lovely and you already know it, you've seen us, we're together again. The other is a bit of tittle-tattle that shames me but I have to tell it. You know that snotty Maurizio with all the pimples? You won't believe it . . . "

"Don't worry, I'll believe anything."

"Well, several times he's waylaid me and made nasty faces at me. Then, this morning, when he found me alone . . . I don't know how to put it . . . he propositioned me, he waved his purse at me and waggled his tongue. I gave him a kick . . . "

"What d'you expect me to do about it?"

"Aren't you the Grand Vizir around here? Tell Mundula, tell his parents, tell *someone*. At any rate, I've told you."

She gives me a fetching pout but I go on: "If only you knew how many troubles I've got, far hairier than that. We'll talk about it some other time." And I escape at the double.

The fact is I have a great urge to talk to Matilde. There's something fishy about that girl, and I'd like to find out what it is. But just as I am raising my fist to knock (the bell doesn't work, the usual power cut I suppose) a ray of sunlight from the end of the corridor strikes me unawares, and I feel drenched with it from head to foot.

I stand there relishing it, pure in heart. I have always set a lot of store by the miracle of this warm hand reaching out from the heavens, crossing gulf upon gulf of space to touch my skin and caress it with such loving friendship. I have always had this feeling about the sun, that its rays travel for my sake alone, heedless of the leprous globule that rolls around it, spellbound by some inexplicable magnetism. I even wonder that it doesn't rebel, burst the bonds of gravity, and set off trusting to luck across the high seas of the universe, beyond the immeasurable bounds of the furthest quasars . . . Until that happens I am content to bathe my limbs, first on one side then on the other, in the dust-laden nimbus; to observe, like a boy watching the tricks of a kaleidoscope, the whirl of golden motes that rains on my eyes, and does not cease, even if I close them, to seethe beneath my eyelids, coloured by my own blood . . .

As I recover from my momentary bewilderment, "What a fuss about nothing!" I scold myself, according to my habit of scaring off any lofty sentiment with the antidote of irony, and the coarser the better (for vulgarity is the very basis of my character). Leaving, therefore, the recent intimate little scene to its fleeting destiny, that holy spark to sink to the level of a feeble joke, I hereupon rejoin the ranks, dismissing both cabbages and kings, and rap hard knuckles against Matilde's door.

When she opens up, her dressing-gown is half open too. No novelty for someone who has seen her as a sleeping *desnuda*, or *desnuda* wakeful in the secret photographs. To be on the safe side, wishing no intimations, I let my eyes stray no lower than her chin. Indeed, as soon as possible I transfer my gaze to the room at large. And in so doing – the matter had escaped my notice at first – discover that none other than Camillo is seated nonchalantly on a sofa of plainly recent acquisition. Nor are he, nor the sofa either, the only novel furnishings introduced by this girl, now that she has become the mistress of the house. So my eye falls on a number of feminine gewgaws on an occasional table: a little velvety animal, an artificial silk anemone in a pot of sand, a musical-box, a Chinese vase . . . and, finally, a photograph of her, Matilde, with him, Camillo, posed like Hollywood lovers. The work of an anonymous hand, certainly not her brother's.

She tells me the news at once: "We're going to get married."

I don't bat an eyelid. After all, why not? Matilde brings a dowry of the apartment, an established studio, Tir's archives and equipment. The fact that she is shapely does no harm, and I don't know how much it matters to Camillo that she has a bit of a past, even supposing he has got wind of it. Rather a crackpot perhaps, but at a guess a pretty good fellow, in spite of my suspicions at first. A person of strong will and rapacious eye, gifts that beseem a photographer aiming at quality. No reason why he should not inherit the most faithful clients of the firm and give it new lustre.

I hasten to congratulate them, but as I do so I see Matilde unexpectedly blush. Who would have suspected that her skimpy deshabille concealed the sentiments of a Dresden shepherdess? Nor is my amazement at an end: her eyes begin to moisten. "I've always had troubles from life," she murmurs. "Troubles and muddles. Now what I want is the boredom of routine. O for those Easters, those August Bank Holidays, those October outings, vacations at the seaside, church on Sundays, three children!" . . .

Camillo nods approvingly, he seems to be directing her like a traffic policeman with his whistle. Among the curly white hair on his chest I no longer see the pendent that surprised me on the day of the funeral, but I am willing to imagine that he is equally popular with society ladies and the young of the discos.

"Tir would have been pleased," Matilde began again, meekly, and the discussion turns to the dead man and the forthcoming All Souls' Day. She tells us that the corpse, by permission of Donna Marzia, is still a guest in the De Castro family vault, but that soon it will have its own plot, purchased a short while ago with a handful of Treasury Bonds which she had inherited. In fact, why don't I go with them to take a look at the place, to come up with an idea for the gravestone and some decorous epitaph?

I hesitate: death and I are suspicious neighbours. I keep a hawk-eyed watch on him. Careful not to rouse him, to be noticed by him. I know that I am one of the infinite numbers of characters of whom death writes the destiny and hides the figures as does a Persian weaver in his carpets. I know that his work of destruction is no less subtle, dramatic, indefatigable, than is the work of creation over which poets sit stooped beneath the light of their lamps. Every corpse is a page that death delivers to the printers. Most of them are commonplace pages, written left-handed, but others! Others are pieces of sublime sculpture, in which we are both repelled and attracted by the immaculate indecency of being nothing more than pure white stillnesses given to decay. Would you dare to put Ilaria del Carretto, albeit so beautiful in marble carved by the hand of Jacopo della Quercia, on a level with the woman herself in flesh and blood, in the ferocious cold of her last instant of life? I will say more: not even the supreme artist, greatest of the great, can equal death in his work of solemn disembodiment of things, in his patient, affectionate decomposition of every tremor, every error, every heroism of our memory into a polished skeletal perfection. Years ago, I know not whether at Heraclea or at Camarina, I saw under glass the bones of an Ancient, half buried in the same earth that had harboured them for millennia. And I recall how I, in the presence of the impeccable cleanliness of that denuded ruin, yearned for no other destiny for the clot of ephemeral humours that is me . . .

"I'll come along," I said eventually. "I owe it to Tiresias."

I realize that for the first time I have said Tiresias, and restored to him his nickname in full. My thoughts run on his blindness: was it on account of glaucoma, as he claimed, or was it not rather, as in the case of the Seer we called him after, a punishment for having seen a naked goddess bathing? A goddess? His sister? And what sort of epitaph could I think up for one who passed from night into still darker night without a chance of greeting the daylight one more time? *"Hic situs, luce finita"*, as on a sarcophagus of yesteryear. Alas no, for Tir the light had come to an end long before.

"I'd really like to come," I repeat. "When?"

"At once. Just let me get dressed."

Half an hour later we are all three of us crammed together on the bus to the Campo Verano.

At the gates Matilde buys a few flowers for Tir. There follows a long search, even with the help of the gate-keeper, to find the places we wanted on the huge map fixed to the wall. An unbelievable map divided up into tenths, with its alleys and cross-paths that branched out by three and by four. In which cheerful relatives swarmed among the white tombstones with their all-thoughtless bravado at the fact of being alive. Nor does it enter their heads that the lawful lords of the realm are there under their feet, invisible, indifferent, oblivious, and happy . . .

When we get to the purchased plot – a pocket-handkerchief of brown earth – "Alas, poor Tir!" I would exclaim, except for knowing that my companions knew no foreign languages.

We therefore continue with our search for the De Castro family chapel. It is not a hard task, for it is marked out by its singular hideousness. With a host of little peplos-clad angels in dazzling Carrara marble and torch-bearers and broken crosses and darling little cypresses. The interior, by contrast, is austere, inspiring meditative gestures and melancholy sentiments. Here all the niches are occupied, except for one, marked in advance with a white Omega, as reserved for its heiress in the person of Donna Marzia. Tir's coffin lies in temporary quarters on the floor . . .

We feel rather like intruders, as is only natural, and as such we are certainly regarded by the oval portraits of the ancestors, armed as they are with bonnets or side-whiskers, from Sister Crocifissa De Castro (1854–1903) back to the far more wordy noble lord Giuseppe (1713–1779), to whose epitaph I find myself gluing my nose at sufficient leisure to commit it to memory:

> *Frigida Josephi hic lapis tegit ossa De Castri.*
> *Accipe, virgo parens, animam; sate Virgine, parce;*
> *ossaque iam terris coeli requiescant in arce.*

Intruders we feel ourselves to be, and so also would the blind man feel, if he knew of it, in this his cut-price lodging.

Meanwhile Matilde has knelt down beside the coffin and is saying a prayer, she dries a tear, she touches up her ruffled features with a spot of make-up, and says: "We can go now."

"Pity," comes Camillo's voice behind her.

"What's a pity?" she asks over her shoulder.

"That pre-war Kodak, a real collector's item . . . Useless there now, in Bartolomeo's hands, as he wanted it to be . . . "

He waits for us to say something. As we don't, he casually adds: "It would earn us enough to furnish a bedroom."

Matilde's indignation bursts forth in high style, but as for me, I am struck with a sudden idea, as when lightning streaks across the night sky and puts its black Hegelian herds to flight.

"It's there!" I exclaim in triumphant tones.

Questioning looks.

"It's there," I repeat. "VR is there, inside the case of the little Kodak, I'll swear to it."

"Even if it is," retorts Matilde haughtily, "it's all right where it is, that way it's better for everyone."

"Amen," say I, and utter not another word, but from a couple of looks I get from Camillo I sense some spectacular developments.

*Tuesday, September 5th*

Of the events that follow I am loath to speak, but to my deep shame I bear witness to them.

So, the next day it pelts with rain. I spend a long time watching the big drops bouncing off the pavement, and my eyes are darkened and my spirits with them. I stay loafing in bed, just for a change, tired of reading, and my hand strays out to the little radio Tir lent me one of the last days of his life for me to listen to *Il matrimonio segreto*, and that I kept after his death as a souvenir. Since then the batteries must have run down, because it scarcely has time to croak one enigmatic ad, "Pino Silvestre, you are fantastic", before drying up altogether. A comical fantasy pops into mind: that such announcements feed a vast conspiracy transmitting coded messages to its adherents, like the voice of Radio London during the last war: "This . . . is London."

But destiny forces me to get up. A voice outside the door is calling me, a voice I recognize. I open up, and it's Camillo brandishing a key.

"Here it is!" he cries. "I ought to take it up to her ladyship, but first I'm thinking that you and I might make better use of it."

I grasp his meaning straight off, and give him an unconvincing no. He insists: "It'll only take a minute. I get the Kodak, you get VR."

Put in such brutal terms the pact makes sense, or at least seems to do so. "It's profanation of a tomb!" I exclaim, and he, infamous fellow, laughs.

"I've got hammers, chisels, a whole kit to open it and nail it up again. We'll be in and out in a jiffy, and I'll do the whole thing. I only need you as a lookout."

I tell him yes and we start off back to Campo Verano.

I pass over the scene of the sacrilege, I have already slandered myself enough. If it may suffice, and I say it not to acquit myself, but to swathe my guilt in a cloak of forgiveness, I have to say that I saw not a thing. At the cemetery gates my glasses fell off right under Camillo's feet, and from then on, leaning on his arm, all I did was navigate between the blunders of my diopters, worse than Oedipus at the crossroads between Jericho and Kolonos, as the philosopher Placido with surrealistic humour said of Tir.

Such a significant ocular misfortune seemed to me a well-deserved expiation at the moment when I was about to violate the peaceful nullity of my lost friend. An even greater retaliation would be to find the yearned-for ark empty. But it did not fall short of our expectations. Faithful to our agreement Camillo extracted VR from its precious receptacle and with his own hand put it in my pocket. Then he took me by the elbow to the nearest oculist and restored my sight.

But one thing I have to confess: the excitement of the search; the curiosity, not to say the hunger and thirst for knowledge; the delight at having at last caught the elusive fox; my anxiety about my future moves . . . all this jumble of worries, commotions and expectations had given place in me to a dead calm of the nervous system, a downright apathy. What would I find, after all? Frames clipped at random from a pornofilm . . . ? Nor was I particularly allured by the prospect of coming across some dirty pictures of Leah, which would inevitably have debased not only the memory but the vainglory of having held her, panting and docile, in my arms. The truth is that, no longer feeling her presence in my heart, my sole justification for going on the warpath must have been the gesture of handing her over the *corpus delicti*, and after a "thanks a lot – not at all", to go my way in peace and give it not another thought. What else, then? The troupe of actors, celebrated or obscure as they may be, La Badalona and her gang, the two poor country girls, the maleficent satyr Mundula, the prelates or other bigwigs whom I might disclose in the befuddled impudence of their nudity if I chose to inform the police or the front page of the "Spyglass"? Was it not better to leave it in the Limbo of things that never happened and wash my hands of it?

Very well. Or rather, very bad. Because I knew of old that, in working out these arguments in my mind, the more convincing I found them the less I would put them into effect. It is my compelling habit, like a malcontent of olden times, to observe the best and cling to the worst, and not without deriving a certain stupid pleasure from the contradiction. Even pigheadedly piling up valid reasons so as to render my refusal the more sensational.

Conclusion: between the two most trouble-free solutions, to burn the thing or hand it over to Leah intact, I naturally chose to have it developed and take a look at it. I might give it to Leah later on, for her edification and remorse.

I therefore dashed off to Camillo, to ask his help. I found him alone in the darkroom, a dusty and abandoned chamber, since Tir had for obvious reasons been unable to use it after he lost his sight. But now, thanks to Camillo, back in working order in view of the imminent re-opening.

He wasn't surprised to see me. In fact he was clearly expecting me, and had been busy tidying up trays, acids, solvents, and the whole arcane mechanism that goes to work the magic of photographic reproduction. When I entered the darkroom it seemed like a cavern for black masses. Total darkness except for a faint half-light from one wall, like the glimmer of a lighthouse seen from a sailing ship. I was intrigued by a large oblong table scattered with cutting implements, little bottles, tissues and sundry trifles, more like a dissecting table than a craftsman's workbench, as far as I could see by the light of a sudden ray that pierced the room when Camillo on his way out pushed the curtain aside for a moment, only to let it fall again at once.

When he returned and got down to work, I from my neutral corner watched him with disgruntled impatience. Although I was expecting it, and indeed had myself requested it, his use of chemicals to beget a life of shadows, no less miraculous than the Fiat Lux seemed to be at the dawn of time, struck me as a usurpation. For there's no getting round the fact that of all the creative and copulative powers of man, with pencils, brushes, chisels, nuts and bolts, or seed instilled in a womb, the one which seems to me most to transcend the iron laws of necessity is photography, the only one that succeeds in conquering History, in halting Time. A canvas, a statue, a building, these can survive while the waters of millennia flow under the bridges, but they are bound in the end to become rubble, dust, nothingness. Whereas the negative of a photograph retains the manifold, not to say the immortal, ability to come back to life again, as we are told of certain bacteria, trapped in amber or in some prehistoric fossil or other which, if you stimulate them with a certain emulsion, become as sprightly and ferocious as at the very instant they appeared on earth.

Since I had not burnt them, a similar seamless privilege awaited the lewd sequences which, due to the action of the acids, I would see gradually emerge in the developing tray. And I admit that against all expectations I felt beset by no little agitation as I watched the first vague figures detach themselves from the indistinct greyness of the background. It was like being a father present at a birth. Although the real father, Tiresias, we had left down there at the feet of Sister Crocifissa De Castro, with his empty hands crossed on his breast.

One minute, one minute more, and at last Camillo lifted out the first print, still wet, as from the waves a Nereid arises streaming water and seaweed . . . We looked at it eagerly enough but what we saw was anything but a Nereid: no news from Sodom, not a word from Sybaris. Instead, not only in the first shot but also in the others which were gradually becoming visible, before a background of trees and statues, whether at Hadrian's Villa or the Villa d'Este at Tivoli, lo and behold a peaceful party of schoolboys on an outing, photographed by an inexperienced hand, in their black smocks and white cloth collars performing a georgic ring-a-ring-a-roses.

# FOURTEEN

# On the Top of the World and From There on Down

*Tuesday, September 19th*

So we have to start all over again. Or rather, the whole thing's over, as far as I'm concerned. I never want to think again of that goddam VR. If it hasn't been found yet it means it's been destroyed, or that it never existed, or else it's buried somewhere beyond recovery. In any case, as things stand, it can do no good or harm to anyone at all. And may the earth lie light upon it! Nothing for it but to accept the fact and be a little touched by the pictures of Tir as a boy, now after several decades of oblivion emerged from his apprentice attempts at photography; and thereafter to return to my usual "So what's?", even if they are more excuses for indolence than signs of desolation.

Thus, after a few hectic weeks, I revert to my sweet routines, to the wonted cadences of my idle day: reading, listening to music, spying on life outside through my same old belovèd peephole on the world, inventing fictions and fantasies according to whatever is suggested by that bustle of legs to and fro, be they brisk or crippled, martial or sensual, all enlisted to perform the briefest or most elaborate of destinies. I write about them too, pages and pages, out of whim or fancy or to ease the heart. Taking only one eccentric and shameful holiday, of a Saturday evening; when, not from kleptomania, but to allow myself a single breath of the air of the town and the thrill of action, I indulge in lone, larcenous incursions through the labyrinths of the "Rinascente" department stores. Footling, innocent little thefts: toothpicks, cotton-reels, tubes of this and that, mere sleights of hand that I perform with perfect cool, in the spirit of a Commando in enemy territory, to get my own back for the panic caused me by the swarm of humanity and its impenetrable foreignness. There is no greed involved, indeed I sometimes return the stuff I have stolen, and take as much pleasure in my adroitness in restoring it as I did in pilfering it the previous Saturday.

Following my example, Flower City also appears to have recovered its own kind of sluggish quietude. I now meet practically no one during my rambles up and down the stairs and along the interminable corridors. I have mentioned more than once that here the liveable apartments are few, and fewer still those actually lived in. So that in the two mammoth structures, and especially in the "Sunflower", there are whole strings of rooms with gaping apertures lacking window-frames, through which zoom gusts of wind as bracing as in any meadow, while swallows, pigeons and magpies wing their way in and scatter the place with feathers, excrement, dried and stiffened corpses.

During one of these perambulations up and down and round about I have an unexpected encounter: it is with Pirzio Ravalli dragging a chair, one of those from the storeroom, one of the fifty-two or fifty-three or fifty-one, or however many there were.

He is not humming to himself as he usually does, but assuming a stern, professional expression. To my affected look of surprise he replies curtly "Homicide Squad", as if I haven't known it for quite a while, and as he has seen Lieut. Colombo do on TV he produces a warrant card which I don't even glance at. Then: "Mum's the word, you haven't seen anything."

I'm tempted to laugh, I know all about that chair. But I go along with him: "Silent as the grave, I promise. But where are you taking that chair? I'm responsible for the equipment . . . "

He takes me seriously: "It's evidence, I'm distraining upon it for a comparison. That is all I can tell you." And off he goes, strutting like the painted peacock.

I've had too many sleepless nights, so I take a sleeping-pill and drop off at once. And after a long time without dreaming I once more dream an old recurring dream. It is always the same except for a supporting character who changes every time. I have always been unwilling to tell other people what I dream, convinced as I am that it might be used against me, but this time I want to see if, translated into words, it acquires meaning or loses it.

I seem to be walking to and fro in front of a princely palace, its vast doors flung wide and beckoning and no sentries in sight. As soon as I cross the threshold a great carpeted staircase, huge basketfuls of flowers on every step, seems to be awaiting me. I start to climb. Suddenly, out of nowhere, two footmen plant themselves before me and load my back with an enormous cardboard parallelepiped, packaged and tied up, commanding me to drag it. Where to? They don't tell me, but wave vaguely towards somewhere above. Slavishly I obey, groping around the bale for grips that will help me to lug the thing along. I resort to a cord made out of a strip of black velvet torn from a curtain and twisted round the base of the thing to act as a sort of pulley, but at the very moment I get my fingers round the bottom corners a tongue of dark warm liquid makes my hands slithery. Well, if this isn't blood! I am not all that horrified, being used to such things by now, when the bale splits open and from inside, as from an Etruscan sarcophagus at Vetulonia, there bursts a corpse with its knees drawn up to its chin, and between its shoulder blades, melodramatic, the haft of a paperknife. While the corpse lies limp in my arms, and I come almost nose to nose with that bloodless face, a bell rings in my memory and, deformed as it may be by a ghastly grimace, it is the face of young Cesare.

This, for me, after my father and Tir, is the third time I've been on touching terms with a corpse, to do what I liked with it, and I am struck once again by the obtuse, dislocated malleability and docility of the dead, their seeming to be without joints or points of resistance. As if made of wax, or plasticine. Then I tell myself that it is not so much life that is rich, as death that is crammed with possibilities, polysemants, comings and goings, decantations . . .

I hoist Cesare over my shoulder, gushing blood as he is, meaning to carry him bodily, but I can't do it. I have to lay him down and haul him by one foot to the top of the stairs, where I collapse on the last step with heaving breath and thumping heart, as always after one of my night terrors. To help me recover I distract myself by looking at the pictures on the walls: strangely modern for surroundings resembling Versailles or Sans-Souci. And odder still is the fact that they are blatant fakes, starting with the De Pisis right in front of me: a ceruse shell on an inexistible beach beside a sea daubed by a bungler. The sort of stuff I used to flog at one time. False, true. True, false. Facts, fantasies. Who says that facts are tenacious? Nonsense, they soon fade away. But, thinking again, that's not true, they dig their heels in, they never give up, they fight like mad. They rise from the dead. And a corpse is a fact, even if it is a fact that does not rise again . . . Yes, but what about you, Cesare? After the ides of March the calends of December? What a vital sloth is death . . . While life is such a funeral . . . Ever pestilent sore and recurring venereal ulcer . . . *Hominum divomque voluptas*, Venus . . .

You will already have understood from these scraps of twaddle that I have left deep sleep to enter a drowsy state that is always for me a muddled, happy condition to be in, comparable to the ecstasies of saints and sibyls. In a minute a drench of cold water will dissolve it.

For conscience' sake I ask after Cesare, although I don't believe in telepathy. Matilde, with exhilarating indiscretion, tells me that the lad is fit and well and working in the orphanage kitchen garden while looking for something better. Camillo would willingly have taken him back into the studio, but she didn't want to. The boy was growing up, and showed signs of being cheeky and uppish. About such things she will stand no nonsense, she wants her employees to keep their hands to themselves and get no ideas about her, especially now that she's setting up house . . .

God bless you, brazen young Matilde, but I'm glad for Cesare that my dream is not about him but alludes to someone else whom I don't know. I seek enlightenment from Placido, who is good at reading these obscure messages in the tea leaves of the consciousness and showing them to be harmless. The chance falls pat, for it's ages since I had a chat with the philosopher. As we neither of us have a telephone we use the intercom when we want to arrange a meeting. This time we fix it for midday up on the flat roof, if the weather is fine.

Fine it is, and at once, without a word, it comes to us naturally to lean on the wall and look out over the city. On this belvedere there is no longer any trace of viewing telescopes for tourists or tenants on permanent holiday, but in its spacious and impressive emptiness the place has the look of a uniformly sun-struck parade ground. There's complete silence up here, save for a constant breeze that vibrates the television aerials. And how tiny the cars look, nose to tail in the "Corso" or shooting along the traffic-free sidestreets; and how more minute still are the rare pedestrians lost in that enormous maelstrom! We are really at the top of the world, at least for one like me who has never been on a genuine skyscraper, and the tone of our discourse is in consequence elevated.

"The dream you had," says Placido, "like all the excretions resulting from the ingestion of rotten fish, is a line of limping, choliambic verse, a stick which Lucifer in his envy has chosen to poke between the spokes of pre-established harmony. Dreams, in fact, are nothing but embellishments, trickeries, mirrors to fool only inexperienced larks. Chaos – and don't you forget it – is simply an illusion, a veil of paradox to conceal the sublime abscissas and ordinates of universal symmetry . . . "

"A put-up job, in fact?"

"Only for a while. Eventually, as Genesis assures us, God intervenes and breathes upon the face of the waters to separate them from the dry land, confining the whirlwind of Hellzapoppin' in the prison of the straight and narrow."

I have to laugh, hearing him talk like this. Just to think how often he has made fun of the Creation, even defining the Big Bang as God's fart. I'm accustomed by now to these changes of humour, which make him propose conflicting concepts every day without any fear of contradicting himself. I imagine he's pleased with himself for being able on alternate days to play the parts of Defender of the Faith and devil's advocate, an apologist now for the police, now for the swindlers. This morning, at any rate, the air feels too good for him to be tempted by the abyss.

"In your dream," he continues, "there float the semblances of a desire and a terror. Unrecognizable, of course. Reduced to mere fumes, to faeces. You will never know what they are unless you see them blossom into a limpid gesture, a lucid thought."

I scarcely listen to him, knowing that next time he will say exactly the opposite and will himself provide the most devastating objections. I may add that what he says is born of the ingenuousness of the self-taught. Although he boasts the title of Professor, he was a professor of the old school. He never spent a penny to purchase Jung or Lacan . . .

As I myself am ignorant of them I don't risk putting my foot in it, but try to change the subject by telling him of the book I mean to write.

"You too?" he says. "Like me?"

It is my turn to be surprised: "Quite a coincidence, two writers in the same block of flats. In fact three, counting Crisafulli. We could found a branch of the Writers' Union."

"Why not? But don't be too bowled over. Three out of fifty or a hundred people . . . We're well below the national average . . . "

"Right, let's make a pact. I won't read you my things and you won't read me yours."

He appears not to have heard me, for he draws about a dozen sheets of paper out of his pocket. "Chapter One," he announces. "The title is *The Death of Narcissus*."

"O no!" I object. "Not Narcissus again! Who will rid us of these Greeks and Romans?"

Like talking to the wall. He clears his throat and starts in: "This is the story of the death of Narcissus as told to me by an old man when I was a child."

A pause. Then: "At that time there were more trees on the earth than men. Trees and waters running under the trees, into which every so often a leaf would fall. The clouds in the sky would play at taking on the shapes of the strangest animals . . . "

He broke off abruptly, seeing a person emerge from the stairwell.

"One of these days I'll let you read the rest."

The person in question is from the paper, one Gabba, the most odious of the lot. One who, if what they say is true, went to bed with my wife Rosa after I left her. A gross fellow and a bully. I can't think why Bendidio sent him instead of Bollocks.

"I've been looking for you everywhere," he pants. "I came up here out of desperation."

The three of us descend together, but before he reaches his floor and gets out of the lift Placido finds time to whisper in my ear: "I myself am Narcissus."

I can well imagine what Arcangelo Bendidio is sending his most resolute emissary to tell me: that I've bogged down, I haven't sent a line of copy; that he'll make me cough up that miserable advance he paid on my forthcoming bulletins from the "theatre of operations"; and in fact that I am an absolute rogue and a traitorous sponger.

Not that he's altogether wrong. I do have things to tell a newspaper and I did take the money. But I'm content with things as they stand, that what happens does not become common knowledge, but continues to occur before and around me like an animated cartoon or a puppet show. In which, while listening to the voice, you see the lips inert in a wooden face, and the limbs moving pretty much at random as the strings are pulled. Therefore the answer is no, and I deliver it to Gabba with such furious scorn that he can think of no better response than to grab hold of me and shake a fist under my nose, before repulsing my feeble reasonings by simply shoving me away.

No, the matter is closed. But I rub my hands with glee as I think of Rosa, and whom she's stuck with. For my own satisfaction I leaf through the notebook containing the seven unknown factors, which I've been neglecting ever since. No doubt about it, right now I have to admit that at least four out of the how's and why's have found an answer. These are: the manner of the revelry, orgy or black mass as maybe; the venue in which it took place; the part played in it by the late Ersilia and the living Dorotea, as well as the whole of the Badalona coterie; the part played by that chair, incongruous as a dog in church . . . The fifth question, that of how Tir died and why, is still in mid-air. And finally there are two completely unresolved problems: the whereabouts of VR and what I ought to do . . .

I'm brought to my senses by a squeaking noise. Once again, either in my head or some invisible crack, there is a mouse complaining. Of hunger? Or is it hurt? Is it caught in a trap? I'll end by believing the Garaffas, man and wife, about their visions of tiny creatures and predictions of imminent collapse. It is often stupid people, as well as children and virgins, who are the most soothsaying soothsayers . . .

As for the dreaded dilapidation of the building, I'm concerned about the furtive meeting between Mundula and the experts from the Town Hall, which I overheard the day before yesterday. There's something going on, quite a few of us know it, but maybe that mouse knows most of all.

And in fact something really is going on, and I am the first to have news of it. On my private screen I see two pairs of policemen's trousers marching swiftly towards our hall door. At first I pay scant attention, the street is public and it's reassuring to have it trodden by boots of public Law and Order. If anything they induce a fleeting reflection on the connection between a monk and his habit. I ask myself, that is, how far the colour of the material, the quality of the wool, the cut, the pleats, possess the power of positive identification, like the pin-striped suit of a Mafia boss or the peaked cap of a mere hired assassin. I would like to look this up in my old Laterza edition of *Sartor resartus*, but I'm very much afraid that it got lost amongst Rosa's lovesick muck. Apart from which . . . but here I must break off, for after the regular fifteen-minute interval Act Two is beginning, and this time there are not four legs but six, there being added, between the former pair, the trousers of Mundula, beige in colour and completed by white socks and Timberland shoes with built-up heels. Am I right? Could I be wrong? In amazement and dismay I tear outside to make sure, but the trio is already a long way off, in a Black Maria, I am informed by the newsvendor across the street. Who gives a shrug and points a thumb at the banner headlines of an evening paper – not, alas, the "Spyglass": *THE ILLEGAL BUILDING RACKET. OFFICIALS AND LANDLORDS ARRESTED. CORRUPTION CHARGES EXPECTED.*

"Oops!" I exclaim after the manner of Bendidio, and go back to my den. It's too late to talk it over with the other tenants, all I can do is find myself something to eat. It's late and I'm hungry. I meet Pirzio, suitcase in hand and humming the words "mission accomplished." I step to one side and give him a slight bow, disliking him more than ever. He very kindly stops to inform me: "You'll read all about it in tomorrow's papers. Mundula has confessed. He was importing the stuff, peddling it, using it himself and corrupting officials. For me this means promotion."

I give him another bow, take my leave and go upstairs to Adele's place. She always puts me aside an egg and a helping of salad for my solitary suppers. I find her in her little room, festooning the wall with bunches of black grapes strung together, like clusters of black pearls, a gift from her brother in from the country. She is a timid, freckled, skinny little thing with pale, bespectacled eyes. If I didn't know her background I'd imagine she was a bookish student. But on the contrary she's a simple country lass who, in terror of Mundula, would occasionally fall back on me for the comfort of some time off or a tip, as a truant student relies on a venal porter to sign him in as present. She

shares the housework with another girl, but only she spends
the night in the building, in a little den on the first floor. There
I find her now, receiving a mildly affectionate welcome and, from
a cage, the song of a canary.

I tell her nothing about Mundula. When she opens her
door she is already too upset about what she has heard from
the greengrocer about a huge strike tomorrow with ominous
intentions, though she hasn't gathered exactly who is striking
for what and against whom. All they said was that tomorrow
there'll be hot goings-on in the "Corso" which runs right past
the building, and that it's a day that will "make history". She
pronounces the word history with open-eyed, childlike enquiry.
It's obvious that history to her is much the same as geography,
and she can't make head or tail of it. I explain nothing, say nothing, but I do wonder why, with all these dramatic happenings,
Bendidio is still interested in the crime pages. I have my meal
along with the girl, in silence but with inner misgivings. When
I get back to my room, and its total darkness, I am struck by
something quite new: the silence of the pavement on my usual
viewing-screen, as if time were suspended. Silence and absence
of life, broken only for a moment by some scurrying footsteps.
No swishing of tyres, no throbbing of engines, nothing but
a distant rumble of tracked vehicles or something of the sort.
Then flashes like lighthouse beams suddenly strike through the
air. An instant later the pavement is grey and lifeless again. I am
reminded of watching the film of the first moon-landing years
ago. Well, the street this evening has all the desolation of a
long-dead heavenly body. What it adds up to is that a curfew is
in force, imposed and instinctively, prudently accepted.

If this is the case Adele has understood rightly, and in vain I
shake Tir's little radio in the hope a last drop of juice will enable
me to hear something. I could, and for a moment the temptation

is strong, ask for info at the "Minibar" opposite, but I don't wish to broadcast news of storms of which I have in fact only three faint indications: the gossip of a char, the haste of some footsteps, the alarm of a mouse in its mouse-hole.

We'll see tomorrow. A night soon passes.

I wake at dawn to a monotonous Niagaran roar. Together with a confusion of voices, in tones ranging from the wrathful to the conversational, from the wheedling to the imperious. With my faithful rod I draw aside the curtains and see a forest of men's legs, performing inexplicable motions, now forwards now backwards, like troops on manoeuvres obeying a series of orders.

I would like to go on looking and try to understand all this, but some sharp reports ring out, and the mass of truncated bodies above me hesitates a moment then turns in the act of flight, unless it is pursuit. I hastily close off my spyhole: I'm scared. So something *is* up, Adele was right. Is it a revolution? A restoration? I have nothing to hope for from either, I who have chosen to live in a bog, I who have completely repented of any passion or participation to fall back on my irrevocable "So whats?"

However it goes, whoever wins, they'll shoot me and they'll have had seventy times seven reasons for doing it . . .

Footsteps pounding outside. They've been quick off the mark. Two, three hard, impatient bashes on the door which, scarcely latched as it is, gives way before I have time to get up and open it. The overalled men who enter scarcely give me a glance, laden down as they are with cine-cameras. They start shifting around the few sticks of furniture. I protest for the sake of protest and all the answer I get is "We fixed it up with the big chief." This intrigues me and instils in me a mite of suspicion. Ten minutes later and all is clear, laughable and disappointing: they are a camera crew, the street has been blocked off since yesterday evening, cleared and put at the disposal of directors, actors, hordes of extras, lighting equipment and film-company vehicles. They'd made their agreement with Mundula, who hadn't been able to let us know for reasons only too obvious. And as for Adele, the poor girl had got the wrong end of the stick. Here in front of our building, and in the building itself, they are just making a movie of a revolution, something as silly as that.

# FIFTEEN

# The Crunch

*Thursday, November 22nd*

When I was a lad I loved the sound of the rain. Now no longer. It affects me like a beggar whining outside the door, a voice cutting through the air like a fingernail scratched across a taut silk umbrella, a thing to set your teeth on edge. I shall have to get used to it, now that week by week we are nearing winter and the year's end.

Yet I approach the end of the year with sinking heart. Even now I am repelled by the ritual emotionalism, the fir trees laden with glittering baubles, carols and hugs and kisses, trumped-up jollity . . . and wet boots to and fro right by my window. I'll draw my curtains, stay indoors. Avoiding the garish "Corso" with its fatuous glare of neon, I shall be free of the endless wail of bagpipes, the Santa Clauses, the roast-chestnut vendors . . . that feeling of hypocritical immortality that unfailingly returns to hoodwink us every time. For a year now I've taken to composing verses on the subject, and have made a version for every tenant in the building, plus one for Rosa, poor semi-widow and sad traitoress that she is, and I sent it to her on New Year's Eve. Starting off with a whole inventory of jeremiads, it ends up – to sweeten the pill and not appear as some sort of jinx – with a homily of bogus hopes. Hereupon I quote you the lot, to make amends, or else, if you prefer, by way of sceptical good wishes:

### NEW YEAR LETTER

Time, O time, ever beginning anew . . .

They say that repetita iuvant;
that the second kiss is more skilful than the first,
that the encore of a happy moment
savours of a honey unnoticed that first evening . . .
But the incoming year with its hoarse oliphant
to blare at our eardrums with
the umpteenth Roncesvalles,
to swell the rivers and denude the trees;
the year that in the bathroom mirror shows
an ever-whitening beard to a sluggish razor;
the year that grows on itself with greed of numbers,
gobbling up the calendar which plays
the recidivous blues of Nevermore
who dares say it deserves a welcoming kiss?
who could swear that it won't be the worst of all?
Misfortune redoubles, repetita non iuvant.
And yet . . .
And yet in the arcane lottery of the Possible
between the dice and chance the game's still open:
the womb of the loam swells with unwonted flowers,
moons never seen before will flood the sky;
in a garden two young people
will tell each other their names and telephone numbers,
astonished to find these names are Eve and Adam;
passing beneath our windows
will come a blind man selling almanacs
to urge us to go on living . . .
Let us believe in him this one last time.

Now then, did you take note of the motto? It is a variation on that line about the sea that I never weary of trying to translate. A variation, however, that makes an impossibility look possible. For time is not permitted either to begin or to end, still less to pause. Whereas the sea *is* so permitted, as also are we, in these our corresponding, proverbial stores of feeling and memory. We too are waves, that ebb and flow, die and are reborn elsewhere. Or else the shifting links in a prodigious chain that some sorcerer's apprentice clumsily ravels and unravels in the silence of eternity . . .

With suchlike philosofarting I fill up the morning, not without pocketing a few smug coins of comfort, now that peace has returned to the building. Learning of Mundula's arrest, the big boss "Jupiter" Cacciola cabled to say he'd be arriving on the next available flight and that in the meantime I was promoted on the spot as sole administrator of the dump, and should rush out and plaster FOR SALE notices all over the facade. Of course you could count the remaining tenants on your fingers, all of them gleefully in arrears, especially Bisceglie, whose enthusiasm may be judged from the trumpet solos that, from his modest lodging, he broadcasts to all twelve storeys.

This alone would be sufficient indication of the lack of authority. But the place is disturbed by other signs and portents. Signora Garaffa has again started to see or to dream up rats as big as rabbits strolling around her room, while I in person, in the middle of the corridor, have come across a turd the same colour as the brown-painted wainscot: of human making, I fear, and to be attributed to one of the three boys, either as an anarchic insult or due to impelling necessity. Finally – and this gives rise to the most sinister conjectures – Adele has shown me, hidden among the rubbish, an open clasp-knife, with a blade stained brown, either with rust or with blood.

A false alarm, probably. In any case, after such a turbulent parenthesis, I intend never again to leave my state of happy self-imprisonment, far less unpleasing, I assure you, than the fate of the most distinguished sailors abandoned on islands, be they Philoctetes, Ben Gunn or Robinson Crusoe. I repeat to myself the famous saw "God helps those who help themselves", and seek no aid but in my own resources. I have a small saucepan, a spirit-stove, a paraffin lamp, as well as a handful of candles for emergencies such as stormy weather or the predictable event of the light being cut off, there being so many bills outstanding.

How to pass the time is no longer a problem: no longer as Bendidio's special correspondent but as a chronicler, a spectator-cum-actor, novelist of the events I have so far observed or experienced in person, manipulating them just enough to turn them into a kind of rhapsody in black, of which I already have clear in mind both the outline and the execution, including the impeccable final loosing of all the knots left in a tangle. And resisting the temptation to provide the boat with a leak that would cause it to sink like a stone, leaving my foeman-reader to drown in mid-passage.

How many times, in like manner, have I thought of leaving my life halfway through, ending it with a resounding pistol shot. So greatly do I suffer the penalty of being gaseous and divided against myself, a farrago of shreds and patches of a man, mottled like marble composite.

O how I envy the characters in great works of literature, consistent, clarified, solid, though of no more bodily substance than an angel or a phoenix. Whereas I, though having my generous supply of red corpuscles, a superabundance of neurons and muscles, a legitimate entry in the parish register, and a conscience, and a past . . . yes I, the more I delude myself that I am alive, the more I melt away, waste away, evaporate through every pore . . .

Water in a sieve, my life has been. Or, as that film put it, tears in the rain. And to think that so often, as I said, I have wanted to get free of it, to rebel against the edicts of the light just as one leaves a boring lecture or dodges a fractious taxman. To sever, to surcease, has always appeared to me the supreme panacea, inconclusiveness is my vocation. If not, more humbly, the only ruse left me to hide in safety from the freemasonry of the living . . . Never, never, in my small inmost soul, will I cease to repent of that one and only non-interruptus that came over me with Rosa. Whence came ye, aborted child, rejected appendix of thyself, spewed-out, unborn pseudo-me! . . .

Reader, I now pick up the threads again. Please bear with me: these aerial sideslips of mine, this insolent assumption of conferring armorial bearings of universal desolation on my own personal marasmus, enable me to let some steam off my ill-humour, like home-made substitutes for electroshock therapy. But that doesn't mean I wish to wriggle out of our specifications and terms of contract, I am a man of honour. But, reader, lend me a hand. In twenty pages time, or even ten, we must take leave of each other. And contrary to all my hopes or expectations, instead of recovering I seem to be worse than ever. All right, I promised you a story that went like clockwork but, as you see, my platoon of puppets are all flat on their backs on a bed of thorns with their guts hanging out. Nor do the figurines of my crazy peep-show manage to pass through the eye of the needle . . .

VR, for example, that intolerable roll of film. Which, with the end drawing near and me having the contractual obligation to discover its whereabouts, I now see taking on real substance for me while hinting at something else, and now becoming an elusive mirage, the jackpot-winning ticket on the pools, the map of Captain Kidd's treasure, the Holy Grail . . . Even its final destiny is in doubt, oscillating between a nine-column headline on the front page of the "Spyglass" and a drop through a manhole into the depths of the Cloaca Maxima, greatest of Roman sewers, where no one will ever find it. Will someone please explain the meaning of this? Excess (or dearth) of imagination? Congenital disbelief in ectoplasm and UFOs, no matter how frequently photographed? In a word, now that the moment has come to fit the fragments of the puzzle together and make some sense of it, why do I insist on suppressing or distorting some addendum so that the sum never comes out right?

Another example is Leah. It was not part of the plan, that I should fancy her, I let myself be waylaid in the course of writing. Until, from the wax doll who figured in the rough version, it came naturally to me to sweeten her into a loving and desirable ewe lamb. But behind her the rest of the cast, every blasted one of them, has mutinied and spawned beneath my pen-nib, they draw up in a Theban phalanx and seem to have it against me. So do events. Which suppurate into tumescent swellings, too much proudflesh, and I can't cope with it. Dear reader, I had no wish for this. All I wanted was to devise a paper maze, a serio-comical scenario of hidden quotations, explosive of course, but no more so than a firecracker or a bursting balloon. Together with a contemplation of death, but cross-eyed, to have a good laugh at it and get it off my chest. My only commitment is to tie it all up at the end. As if that were as easy as winking . . . As if it were easy in the face of every Thalidomide abortion, every stray bullet, every mole-cricket (*Grillotalpa grillotalpa*, most gruesome of insects), or any of the monsters at Bagheria or Bomarzio . . . in the face of all unreasonings, misreasonings, deformations . . . of all the uprooted vines and meteoropathies of the Event, to oppose the grammar and grey matter of Sufficient Reason . . . As if it were easy with the short sight

I'm cursed with to correct all the errata I've managed to strew throughout the printer's dummy that has been my life . . .

Damn it, I've done it again. But when I really take a run at it, checking myself requires a degree of heroism I don't possess.

Though if only you knew what benefit I get from these unbridled gallops, neck and neck with the wind; spasms of self-consciousness which I exploit to give freedom of speech to my writerly tribulations. I return from them cleansed and lucid, ready to obey the rules as scrupulously as a novice on Mount Athos. And the rules now require me to take the reins in hand again. We begin with an encounter under a single umbrella, just outside the building. It is Lo Surdo who offers me shelter. He has obtained a pass to leave prison for an hour or so and visit Crisafulli in hospital, where he is on his deathbed and asking to see him. He invites me to come with him. Why not?

We find the patient in a less damaged condition than we had feared. He has got over his heart attack and he plays the fool more foolishly than ever. Except that his language has come down a notch or two, as if his bombast of the other evening was the pin that bursts the bubo. So much so that his gestures and jargon, though remaining delightfully absurd, emerge with restrained and laconic simplicity, such as is required to appeal to the innocence of the nursing sisters. Since he doesn't read newspapers and has scarcely heard of television, but is mad about comic-strips, he knows nothing about our recent legal adventures and we don't say a word about them. He, on the other hand, shows us a cartoon, and in doing so lets a tiny receipt coupon escape from between the pages and flutter down onto the sheet: Left Luggage Office, Rome Terminus, number such and such. It's our turn to be surprised. "Is that yours?" asks Lo Surdo, and proceeds to tease him: "What are you hiding, eh? Stolen diamonds? Love letters? A woman you've murdered and chopped to bits?"

Crisafulli pulls a face, playing dumb. But then he slaps his brow and cries: "Ah, Tir! Pinocchio. Braille. Dropped paper. Returned book." I don't know why, but his illness has caused him a diminution of his verbal circuits to the lowest possible denominator, so that he talks like Morse Code, or like a poet, but in my view with absolutely logical consequence. Lo Surdo is uncertain at first, but after a while my translation convinces him. This is the way it must have all happened: mad about any sort of cipher writing, Crisafulli pays Tir a visit and sees a copy of *Pinocchio* in Braille, so he borrows it to take a look at without telling the owner. While he is poring over it out falls the Left Luggage receipt, which he picks up and absent-mindedly pops in among his comic books, so that we now find it quietly tucked in between Archibald and Petronilla.

My heart starts racing. Got it! I close my fist on the receipt and change the subject. But the madman, full of suspicion, demands, "Where is it?"

"I'll give it to Matilde," I tell him. "She comes in to everything, including books and receipt slips."

But Crisafulli is already thinking of other things, his interval of semi-lucidity must have passed, along with regular breathing. We see him half sit up in bed, in the long night-shirt that no one has succeeded in making him forsake for the regulation hospital pyjamas, and hear him gasping frantically into an imaginary megaphone:

"Your Royal Highnesses, Most Honourable Senators, I declare you my prisoners. For the next twenty-four hours you will not leave these premises, all passes are suspended save permission every four hours for the lesser business in the bog. You laugh? In a short while you'll be weeping . . . "

"No one is laughing, Signor Crisafulli," Lo Surdo assures him affectionately. "No one at all."

But the spectre is not even listening. With his bony, naked arms protruding from his sleeves he accompanies scraps of unintelligible words, probably the very ones he didn't have time to recite on the evening of the catastrophe.

"I will accept no arguments. I claim the right to die, and a safe-conduct which you will vote on and sign this instant. And not only for myself. The populace is in revolt, they are besieging Parliament. Vast hordes are swarming in from all the provinces of the Empire . . . Don't you hear the marching steps, the drums and trumpets, the outcry down there in the streets? I myself, as God is my witness, I myself in this same place in one minute's time will die by my own hand . . . "

With forefinger and thumb he made a clumsy mime of firing a revolver, then fell back exhausted on the pillow and asked for a cigarette. Before we could make any reply he had already fallen into such a state of deep unconsciousness that we didn't know whether it was the beginning of a stretch of regenerating sleep or of an irreversible coma. As we left Lo Surdo asked me, "What d'you aim to do with it?" as he saw me clutching in my fist the miraculous voucher.

I didn't answer. I was thinking of the inevitable disenchantment that follows upon any Open Sesame or Golden Fleece. I almost said "So what?" and smiled to myself: it was hard to slough off that habit.

"What to do with it?" I echoed Lo Surdo's question and meanwhile rummaged amongst my schoolboy reminiscences for the conclusion of the voyage of the Argonauts. My mind was a blank, although I vaguely remembered that Jason didn't come to a happy end . . .

In any case I dash to the station. I am alone in the taxi; Lo

Surdo has had to report back, his pass had nearly expired. I spend a long time hunting for the Left Luggage Office, and when I find it it appears to be swarming with maddened travellers bitten by the tarantula of constant movement, incorrigibly love-sick for Elsewhere, convinced that it is better far than Here.

I have to wait for the crowd to thin out, and then, in return for a modest fee, and with a casualness that takes my breath away, I come into possession of a package that for size and shape cannot but fulfil my expectations. I open it with trembling fingers and instantly wrap it up again. Yes, we've got it. This time we're in luck. Like the saint whose name I bear, Doubting Thomas, I have at last seen and touched the thing itself, and have no further doubts. I slip VR into my pocket and hold a caressing hand over it to make certain every moment that it's still there. Then, as is my wont, while I make my way back on foot I take stock of the whole story and my own part in it. When at last I drag my weary bones back home, my conclusions are as follows: I could 1) examine the evidence and give a report of it in a shattering article that would make me famous in twenty-four hours; 2) not look at it but give it to Leah out of gratitude and as a parting gift; 3) look at it and use it feloniously to blackmail La Badalona; 4) not look at it and turn it over intact to the police; 5) look for the nearest dustbin and simply drop it in . . .

These five hypotheses give rise to five possible modes of conduct all equally repellent to me. Therefore the customary melancholy phenomenon manifests itself in me: the more that, making a sacrifice to the spirit of geometry, I mark my blackboard with rational arrows indicating my behaviour and prepare a tableful of choices, the pros and cons calculated to the nth degree, the more I haver like Buridan's ass between this delectable morsel and the next, while I perish of confusion and starvation.

In the meanwhile I drop off into one of those lethargies that we often mistake for sleep, but are really scarcely more than daydreams. Then . . .

Then I hear a crunching sound, as of bones in the grip of an immense hand. Followed by several seconds of unnatural, ominous silence. What on earth is happening? A great roar, a sort of miles-long bellyrumble, runs through the innards of the building. Everything around me is lurching this way and that. I don't even have time to realize that it is not an earthquake but a ruinous collapse before the lights go out, I feel a whole mountain settling down above my head. The little window through which a moment ago I saw the skinny legs of an old woman suddenly goes dark. I may be wrong, but I seem to be buried alive in my basement under God knows how many millions of stones. It was no coincidence that among Madame Adriana's Tarot cards was that of the lightning-struck Tower . . .

Needless to say I have written the foregoing words not *during* but *after*, by the light of a candle. In the total darkness surrounding me I groped for one and lit it. After such a crashing and banging all is silent now, not so much as a whisper. Evidently the structure of beams and architraves flopped down on me like a collapsing sail and has settled over my head into a peaceful pile of rubble. I have an insane moment of rage when I think that Engineer Garaffa was right. That ignoramus saw correctly, that those tiny cracks in the cement were not scars but eloquent wounds. Everything here was built on mud and made of mud, not steel and concrete. Now there is nothing for it but to wait in this bubble of remaining air for someone to dig down and find me. Alive or dead? Who knows . . . There must be a mass of great boulders between me and the light. Moreover the likelihood is that the rescuers, unaware of the basement, will start at the top. Trapped to perfection, I shall last as long as this light, or scarcely more, and even it as it burns consumes precious air. Bah, one extra hour is not much of a gain, I prefer to die writing. Telling first of all of my infinite astonishment at having passed so abruptly from the humdrum everyday to the eternal, from tranquil awareness of drawing breath to feeling on my deathbed. Maybe the same thing happens in cases of fatal heart attacks. And in fact a fatal heart attack has struck the coronaries of this building, and with it my own. Now even my pen grows weak, my bloodless, tremulous biro. Acquiescence in my end invades and persuades me like deep sleep. Out, out brief candle, and with you my own brief light; erase the photos of this invented Walpurgis-night, burn this manuscript of mine, in case I don't make it in time, with these withered hands, to hide it beneath my shirt to preserve it, a final reportage from the hereafter for Bendidio's front page . . .

# SIXTEEN

# Epiprologue

Someone at the door. I know who it is even before he enters. He has knocked with the metal ferule of his stick, so it is the tenant from the floor above, Martino Alàbiso, the blind photographer. In reply to my "come in" he pushes open the door and feels his way forward, delving his stick into the air like an oar into water. He knows that from the doorway to my table means five steps down and nine paces forward, and he negotiates them with confidence and caution. Then he stops at the spot where intuition tells him that an empty chair awaits him. He is preceded by a violent wave of eau-de-cologne, which he has a weakness for.

My eyes go straight to his hands: in one of them he is grasping his stick, in the other the manuscript of The Crunch. About time too. It's six weeks since I gave it him for an opinion. I admit that he has had to have it read aloud to him by his apprentice, but all the same he might have been a bit quicker. The long wait has kept me on tenterhooks, as does now his expression, a mixture of embarrassment and severity. I expected no better after the reservations he came up with sight unseen, when I told him that, albeit under a pseudonym, I had chosen him as the hero whose death occasioned the whole sad business.

"Well then?" I ask nervously.

He doesn't stand on ceremony: "Thumbs down. What am I

saying, 'thumbs'? Index, middle, third and little fingers as well. On both hands."

"I wouldn't like to think . . . " I protest, but he doesn't let me finish.

"Yes, I have also a personal grudge to bear. That slander about what practically amounts to incest with a non-existent sister, I who am an only and prodigal son! And then all the rest of it, an incredible Grand Guignol, an insult to a community like ours, so respectable, so middle-class! You've made us into a bunch of eccentrics and delinquents . . . The only things you've described faithfully are your own mental convolutions – and I mean *mental*!"

I make no secret of my disgruntlement. "I am not a photographer," I inform him. "My realm is dreams and tall stories. Reality I use only as a mere pretext, as a match to light the Catherine-wheel of vision . . . Although, worse luck, I am not Honoré de Balzac."

"You can say that again," says he mercilessly. Then he twists the knife in the wound:

"What more do you want me to say? Well, I'll tell you that I'm fairly put off by the shilly-shallying of the writing, now up now down, at one moment gutterpress and the next flights of lofty oratory. An ill-tempered clavier, a karaoke style . . ."

I take the blows, one after another, rebelling in my forum of conscience without uttering a word.

He realizes that he's gone too far, and tries to make amends: "Maybe at a second reading . . . "

His words drift off, he waits. Then, "The fact is, I was hoping for better. The first few pages took me in. But the story of the blind photographer you ought not to have cheapened by putting it in a setting of third-rate bacchanalia. There was – there is – in my condition a metaphor which you haven't grasped. And apart from that the background, the city itself, society, whatever happened to them? Not only the *how* of it, but we don't even understand the where and when and why . . . "

"That may be so," I retort, "but I have always thought it up to the reader to invent these things for himself. My reason for writing was quite different: to overcome anguish with the exuberance of style. And it has worked. Too bad for the others, the great writers. As they write they sicken, while as I write I recover; an age-long insomniac I regain the power of sleep on the pillow of words. In short, the book stays as it is. My only concession is to change your name, if Tiresias doesn't suit your fancy."

I can see him soften. "No, no, I like the name Tiresias. I also like the way I get the hell out of it so early on, it saves me from making even more of a fool of myself. And I'd have had it anyway when it came to the crunch."

"You bet!" I crow at him. "It's an author's privilege to kill whoever he likes and improvise catastrophes. That smash-up, for anyone looking for inadvertent depths, suggests far more than an abuse of building regulations, it foreshadows the collapse and ruin of the century, of the millennium."

"You don't say!" exclaims the blind man sarcastically. "But the sore point is quite different: it's the number and impact of the improbabilities. It's not that I'm mad about literal truth, for after all I photograph darkness, but all the same I prefer what is possible or probable to the improbable or impossible. Whereas in your story there are too many odd coincidences."

I don't want to give in, so I object: "But where in the goings-on of life do we find the borderline between normality and absurdity? Don't you see how surprising things seem when we imagine them, and how natural they appear when they actually occur? Even the most incredible holing-out in one or a cannon rebounding seven times off the cush before striking the second ball, if they really happen on a golf course or a billiard table, why their existence becomes incontrovertible, invincible, historic, and confutes all the more obvious alternatives."

"Bully for you," laughs the blind man. "At this rate we'll end up in the arms of Tertullian. Don't tell me you believe in God . . . "

"That would be the last straw. Except that God is too useful an absurdity for us to discard. You can't deny that you yourself hanker after him. As if you didn't know that when your shutter goes click click at nothingness, it is him that it's trying to catch, or else his stand-in. Who is extremely careful not to blunder into the meshes of your net."

He hesitates, with a gesture he brushes aside the tinge of melancholy irreverence glimpsed in my words, and, after a pause, as is customary in our daily verbal skirmishes: "Leaving out God, who at this point is not pertinent and who, if he exists, can be nothing more than a monstrous computer, I cannot say how amazed I am – if you follow me – at the impudence with which, in your book, things without rhyme or reason masquerade as necessity."

"But that's the way it is in life as well," I murmur. "In which, if you think about it, not only is the exception as plausible as the rule, but every rule is as implausible as the exception . . . "

Martino shakes his head: "An example, give me an example."

"Very well, take my birth, or yours come to that. Think how many hundreds of thousands of thousands of possibilities they had to find a path between, through how many labyrinths they had to find the thread, how many traps they had to steer clear of, to come into existence. What I'm saying is that any happening, great or small, is such a risk as to belittle what we are accustomed to call miracles."

"If everything is miraculous," asked the blind man dubiously, "where does necessity come in?"

"It's the other side of the coin," said I. "As in a two-faced herma. And these two, destiny and chance, so minimal is the distance between them, that they swap over costumes and words like Othello and Iago on the stage, playing alternate nights. But to return to my book . . . "

"The tongue ever turns to the aching book," laughed Martino. "Well, even if I agreed to every word you say, your book wouldn't be any the better for it."

I had to laugh too. "I only wished to defend the principle of incongruity as the prolific driving force of any fiction. To explain to you that whatever in my story might have seemed an extraordinary, disorderly stream of miracles, in reality is no less ordinary and legitimate than the merging of two drops of water on the same leaf."

He remained unmoved: "Rewrite it, rethink it. And change something in the destiny of the character who is me. Even if only to ward off bad luck. I wouldn't like life to imitate art . . . As for the solidity of this building, well, perhaps a check-up is called for. You've put more than one flea in my ear."

At this point there is nothing for it but to go to the cinema.

The cinema in question is a modest one in the outskirts, where they put on blue movies or else, far more rarely, third or fourth showings. Like this evening, when they've announced *The Gardens of Compton House*, a good film according to Placido, who's quite an expert on the subject. He tells me that it touches on subjects that have something to do with the way Martino and I argue about the fine line that divides invention from truth. "A suspect coincidence," grumbles the blind man, when I give him the outline of the plot as far as I know it. But an even stranger coincidence alarms us: across the poster exhibited near the entrance a hand-written strip announces "Cancelled", and in exchange offers a different programme, a classic of the French cinema. I am dumbfounded to observe the well-worn poster of nothing less than *Lancelot* . . .

"Look," I exclaim to the blind man, "it's *Lancelot*, just as in a scene in my book . . . "

At first he doesn't seem put out; in fact he hums a few bars from Verdi's *Ballo in maschera*:

> *Oh che baccano sul caso strano,*
> *oh che commenti per la città . . .*

Then suddenly he has second thoughts, he looks serious: "Incredible, it couldn't be that you . . . "

"What are you thinking of, how on earth could I have known? It's a film made years and years ago. I can't think how they dug it up."

He nods but I see he's bewildered and hostile. We go in all the same and find the show has already started, with the two lovers at a tryst. According to our long-standing agreement, between one dialogue and the next I whisper the essential details in Martino's ear, but pretty soon he shuts me up, all his attention on the sound track, full of neighing steeds, clashing sword blades, the clanging of heavy armour. When it's over he comes back to the strangeness of the coincidence:

"Couldn't it be that while you were writing you remembered seeing a poster for the film on some previous occasion? A case of subliminal suggestion?"

I had put the same question to myself, and in all honesty I answer no. Therefore I put forward a bizarre explanation:

"Might not the characters in a novel be like unborn children, or insects as yet unformed, grubs that long to become living creatures? And the same thing with events. Couldn't my rotten novel have put its finger on the mysterious button that sets Non-Being in motion and turns it into Being?"

"You're showing off," he reproaches me. "It was simply a coincidence and there's an end to it."

So saying he raps with his stick on the pavement. The few spectators are leaving along with us, loudly declaiming their dissatisfaction with the film and longing for pizzas and discos. One couple running for a taxi nearly bowls us over. Left on our own we set off for home on foot, side by side, with me affectionately guiding him with warnings that irritate him, so sure is he of his skill and long experience of walking this accustomed route.

It is therefore with infinite astonishment that I see him suddenly shake off my arm and stride off across the road, three yards before the zebra crossing. Not an instant to rebuke or start after him before I hear, like the blare of the Last Trump, the snarl of a Kawasaki coming from behind me.

"Martino, Tir! Look out!" is my voiceless cry, as I watch the blind man's head practically in smithereens while his body, spread-eagled like a scarecrow's, swirls through space before smashing against the wall, to print a crimson silhouette on the poster for *Lancelot*.

## Dramatis personae

| | |
|---|---|
| Adele | Cleaning woman in the block |
| Adriana della Monica | Fortune-teller, sorceress of high standing. Shares her son Maurizio with her estranged husband on a six-monthly rota. A plump, elderly lady |
| Argiropoulos, George & Constantine | Young Greek twins |
| Argiropoulos, Katina & Demetrios | Parents of the twins George & Constantine, dealers in Oriental carpets |
| Badalona, La | Stately as a Spanish galleon. Runs a drug gang, lives royally on the proceeds |
| Bartolomeo Guelfi | See Tiresias |
| Bendidio | Sicilian newspaperman, Tommaso's ex-boss, gives him a fresh assignment |
| Bisceglie, Johnny | The most insolvent tenant in the block, a jazz trumpeter. Lives on sixth floor |
| Buozzi, Malatesta | Printer, lives with daughter (or step-daughter, or adopted daughter) Leah. Anarchist resigned to bourgeois existence. Lives on first-floor |
| Cacciola, Mr "Jupiter" | Italo-American proprietor of Flower City |
| Camillo, Signor | Ear-ringed ex-partner of Tiresias's |
| Carnemolla, Placido | Retired professor of philosophy. In his 70s. A non-stop talker. Lives alone on the eighth floor |
| Cesare | Tiresias's guide-boy, aged 17, occasional lover of Matilde |
| Crisafulli, Gregorio | Retired thespian, unsuccessful playwright |
| Donna Marzia de Castro | Aristocrat fallen on hard times. Aged c.80. Survives by selling off her heirlooms. Lives alone on the eighth floor |
| Dorotea | Street-girl, companion of Ersilia |
| Ersilia Trapani | Street-girl, dead from an overdose of crack |

| | |
|---|---|
| Flower City | Name of apartment block. Two blocks, in fact, Carnation and Sunflower, but only the former completed |
| Garaffa, Rosalba | Married to Engineer Garaffa |
| Garaffa, Engineer | A man of imperceptible intelligence |
| Gioele | Pirzio Ravalli's lady friend |
| Leah Buozzi | A taciturn beauty, aged 19, lives with Buozzi, Malatesta, who is probably not her father. Is Tommaso's current heart-throb |
| Lo Surdo, Enrico | Lives on seventh floor. Wears white shoes and nut-brown trousers. Ex-owner of paper-mill (torched) |
| Marino, Torquato | See Mariposa |
| Mariposa | Torquato Marino, cross-dresser, plies for hire |
| Martino Alàbiso | Blind photographer, Tiresias's alter ego |
| Matilde | Younger sister of Tiresias. Shares his third-floor flat |
| Maurizio | Son of Adriana della Monica |
| Mundula, Leone | Lawyer and chief administrator of the apartment block |
| *Mus musculus* | Mouse with whom Signora Garaffa keeps reluctant company in her flat |
| Ravalli, Pirzio | Chartered accountant, constantly invisible, with a lady friend called Gioele |
| Rosa Mulè | Ex-wife of Tommaso. Owner of a sports shop |
| Santina | Cleaning woman in the block |
| Tiresias (Tir) | Blind photographer, Tommaso's friend, aged 50. Lives on the third-floor |
| Tommaso Mulè | Janitor of apartment block, ex-journalist, ex-husband, aged 49. Describes himself as urban speleologist. Lives on lower ground floor |